She woke with the sen
she was right...

Casey didn't know how long she'd been asleep. She sat up, rubbing her eyes and staring into the unsmiling face of a man on huge, black and gray speckled horse. For a moment, she credited her imagination. Had she been dreaming? He seemed too big to be real. No, this man's sudden appearance at their picnic in the woods was not a part of her imagination, she couldn't have dreamed up anyone like him.

She looked toward Jake who still slept, curled in a ball, hands clasped beneath his cheek. Nothing would wake her son until he was finished sleeping. Casey leaped to her feet, hands on hips, ready to do battle. With a mouth lined in cotton, she had a hard time swallowing. Her pulses raced, and the vein in her neck throbbed.

He sat easily on the horse. With his dark green wool shirt tucked in the waistband of tight, well-worn jeans and boots firmly placed in the saddle stirrups, he could have stepped from the pages of a western novel. His eyes, the color of coffee, were fringed with sooty black lashes.

Observing the stranger's impassive, stony visage, she worried about Jake. Would he wake up at the wrong time? She wondered what to use for a weapon if she had to.

The man swept off his hat, gesturing with it toward the canyon walls. "This is Tyree land. What are you doing here?" Coming from his wide chest, his voice was deep. Definitely unfriendly.

She hadn't expected anyone to read the love messages she tossed away...but he did.

Recuperating from an abusive marriage, Casey Nichols flees with her asthmatic, six-year-old son Jake to Colorado, hoping to improve his health. She moves them into an isolated cabin on a remote ranch. It's a lonely life, and Casey resorts to putting notes in the ever-present tumbleweeds, casting them to the winds in an effort to ease some of the pain in her heart. But when the poems she thinks will never be read are found by the one person she doesn't want to see them, her whole world is turned upside down.

He hadn't expected anyone to get close enough to hurt him again...but she did.

Matthew Tyree is a reclusive rancher who lost his wife and unborn son in a car accident. Devastated, he has vowed never to love again—a vow he keeps until Casey and Jake worm their way into his heart. But his hopes for a second family are dashed when Casey mistakes his marriage proposal as nothing more than a convenient business arrangement. Unable to express his feelings in the words Casey needs to hear, Matt watches his chance for love crumble like the mysterious poems he's been finding inside the tumbleweeds.

Can these two wounded souls learn to trust again or will their only chance for happiness fade away like love letters cast to the winds?

KUDOS for *Love Letters in the Wind*

Love Letters in the Wind by Pinkie Paranya is a contemporary western romance guaranteed to twirl the lasso of the cowgirl in all of us...no simple hearts and flowers tale. It interweaves real life medical issues with daily existence on a remote western ranch. Supporting characters add depth and provide challenges to Matt and Casey's journey, especially when Casey's past follows her to the ranch, threatening to destroy the new life she's built for her and Jake and any future she'd hope for them with Matt. The heat count on this romance is set to mild, but the romance is strong. Paranya concentrates on the building of trust and the struggles faced by our leads, ensuring a fine romance and a wonderful read. – *Taylor, Reviewer*

Love Letters in the Wind is the heart-warming story of two wounded souls, trying to put the past behind them and start life over. They are afraid to trust and equally afraid not to. A new novel by Pinkie Paranya, the book has a western flavor that I enjoyed very much. It also features an asthmatic six-year-old boy who is just adorable. The plot has some interesting twists and turns that capture the reader's attention and refuse to let go. I was riveted up to the last page, wondering when the hero and heroine would get their heads out of their butts and do the right thing. The characters, as always with Paranya, are down to earth, strong—yet and vulnerable—and totally authentic. Add a strong plot, vivid scene descriptions, and a warm, touching romance and you have another Pinkie Paranya classic. – *Regan, Reviewer*

LOVE LETTERS

IN THE WIND

By

PINKIE PARANYA

A BLACK OPAL BOOKS PUBLICATION

DEDICATION

To my special friends, who have dedicated so much time and love toward the welfare of cats and dogs: June Agur, Sally Smith, Mary Scribner, and Susan Cesarini.

CHAPTER 1

The strong, cold wind from the Colorado plains blew across Casey Nichols' face. She drew the thin windbreaker closer to her body, wishing she had brought warmer clothes with her. Her long, curly hair, torn from the ribbon at the nape of her neck, blew around her eyes, mixing with the tears pressing from under her closed eyelids. She brushed them away with anger, wanting to hide them from Jake. She wasn't weak, damn it, and she wouldn't cry. This journey had to work out for them.

"Ready to send another message?" Jake asked.

They leaned against the porch railing and she bent forward, brushing a lock of blond hair from his forehead. He looked healthier every day they were here.

"You okay, Son?"

He nodded. His huge blue eyes, surrounded by bruised-looking skin, dominated his pale face. A child of six, he looked much younger, and once more, she vowed to do whatever it took to change his condition from sick to healthy.

Since they arrived in Colorado two weeks ago, this game with messages inserted into the center of a tumbleweed was their playtime—a time when Jake could come outdoors and soak up the bright sun and fresh air.

He motioned toward the towering mountains behind them. "Do you miss our house back there?"

Phoenix was inextricably connected to her past and to Richard. She didn't want to be anywhere near her ex right now, and she wasn't about to let Richard's parents track her down before she was ready to deal with them.

She hedged, not sure of how to answer his question. "Do *you* miss it? We're on an adventure now."

"Aren't we supposed to work?"

Casey thought of the ad in the throw away paper that she answered in a rare spontaneous moment.

Groundskeeper wanted for temporary summer work. Live on remote ranch, bonus at end of job if stay the duration.

Maybe it was a tad irresponsible to use her initials when she answered, but it sounded as if this rancher had a male groundskeeper in mind when he ran the ad. The remote part was what drew her to answer.

"We'll have to wait and see what Mr. Tyree wants us to do when he comes home. I think he's probably out there somewhere branding cattle."

"Wow! Will I get to watch sometime?"

Casey smiled. "Can't say for sure," she said, though she doubted it.

She only spoke briefly with Tyree's mother, who seemed to think her applying for the job was hilarious. Not a good sign. Tyree was reclusive, according to his mother, and not at all sociable. She advised Casey to settle into the cabin and her son would come look her up when he got home. Casey couldn't help but feel something else bothered the woman about her son, but if so, she didn't talk about it.

"I've never had a 'venture before, have I?" Jake asked, interrupting her thoughts.

"No, not really." She crumpled the note. "If we fold the paper too neatly, it may fall out," she explained. "It's the same idea as putting a message in a bottle and throwing it into the ocean. A long time ago I read in a book about someone throwing notes away in tumbleweeds. When I saw all the tumbleweeds blowing around here, I remembered that and thought it would be a fun idea for us."

She knew how to express herself on paper. This game of theirs was an outlet—with no strings attached—and no judgments. With every note she sent on its way, it became easier to open her heart. She felt protected, knowing the weeds would crumble to dust along with her poems.

She and Jake didn't need anyone else. They had each other.

Holding the prickly tumbleweed between gloved hands, she grinned down at him. "Are we ready?"

He laughed, a small sound but it made her throat tighten so that she had a hard time swallowing, thinking how long it had been since she'd heard him laugh without coughing.

She tossed the round, dry weed into the ever-present wind. It blew away, rolling, flying past the incline in front of the cabin, with a destiny all its own.

"Goodbye brave message," she shouted. Her words dipped off the ledge and plummeted down the narrow canyon below. Casey straightened her shoulders and tilted her chin. In her thirty-two years, this was the first time she had functioned as the sole caretaker of her own destiny. It felt scary but good. She couldn't be sure if she was enough for Jake, but she wanted to be both mother and father to him.

"What did you call the bushes?" he asked again.

"Tumbleweeds. Remember, I showed you some in the desert book? We had tons of them around Phoenix. I guess we never went out on the desert to look, did we?" There were many things she had never done with Jake. A lot of things to make up for.

"They start out as green bushes, but they don't have many roots, and the ones they have don't go deep. The plants dry, break loose from the soil, and turn into tumbleweeds."

She needed to be a tumbleweed for a while, with no roots to bog her down. Vegetables have roots, and she was through being a vegetable, accepting and yielding.

Jake smiled up at her. "Putting notes inside them kinda makes 'em tumblewords, doesn't it?"

Casey knelt to hug her son close, leaning her head lightly against his narrow shoulder, inhaling his clean, soapy, little-boy smell before he so typically pulled away. She loved his imagination, his quick understanding, and his enjoyment of words. They were alike in so many ways.

"Aren't we lucky? We can use the wind to take our tumblewords."

When Jake grinned, she smiled, feeling suddenly uplifted.

"Where'll it go? I bet all the way to Denver. Is that far?"

"A bit too far, even for this wind, I'm afraid. There'll be lots of cows that might read them—and don't forget the roadrunners, snakes and lizards."

He giggled, lifting his hand to make their high-five sign. They slapped together, she carefully, he with all his strength. "Hey, you're getting better at this. You'll have to go easy on me one day, or you'll hurt my hand."

His big blue eyes searched her face for ridicule. Finding none, he hugged her close. "Love you, Mom," he whispered as if embarrassed to say it out loud.

"Me, too, Son."

Like the child he was, he lost interest in the moment of affection—that she lived for—and ran to the porch railing. "There's millions out there, we'll never run out will we?"

"I doubt it."

"Think someone like a person——will read the notes?" he persisted.

Casey looked off toward the hills, certain she did not want anyone to read her poems. Being alone was what she wanted. Wasn't it?

Matthew Tyree bent low over the saddle to reach the bit of dried brush. "Damned tourists, tossing junk all over the place."

Where the box canyon ended, he figured he would find some strays. Sure enough, as if pretending they didn't see him ride up on the gelding, the young steers chomped the prairie grass. They didn't fool him. He saw the whites around their eyeballs telling him they were primed to bolt and run.

He thumbed his Stetson back from his forehead and impatiently crumbled the prickly brush between his gloves, reaching for the wrinkled piece of paper. It would not have meant much if this had been the first time he saw the littering. Down on the mesa, where he'd been camped out for the past month, rounding up strays, he'd found another bit of paper caught in the weeds and had ignored it as trivial.

But enough was enough. If there was a receipt or a name anywhere, he would call or write the creep——tell him off about littering the prairie. The paper was probably 5x7, white, with the top edged in glue as if the writer had torn it from a stationary tablet. He smoothed the paper across his thigh. It contained a poem, written with a pen in small, tight handwriting.

He studied it for a long moment, surprised at seeing a poem when he expected a store receipt or something way more prosaic and then read it out loud.

"Lost——a dream once young and happy
  "Now embittered——oh so old.
"Lost—a heart once warm and tender
  "Suddenly turned hard and cold.

  "Gone the memories of laughter,
  "No more the kisses, gentle sighs.
"The curtain bringing down the last act
  "Brings to tears, once laughing eyes.

"Life brings fear and sorrow crushing...
  "Doubtful are the roads once crossed.
    "Life goes on——never ceasing...
    "Life goes on——but love is lost."

Matt sat a long while, barely noticing the gelding's restive hooves stamping on the hard desert floor. Where had this come from? The meaning was clear, striking a chord deep inside him that he'd believed buried for good.

He hadn't thought about love in ages, not since Dorothy died. He did not want to now. He was finished with love, had no need for any kind of mushy emotional turmoil at his age. His ranch, his work, was all encompassing, everything he needed. His life satisfied him—damned right it did. He crumpled the note in his fist and almost threw it away, but stopped to smooth it again and stuff it in his shirt pocket. The raw pain in the poem intrigued him. He had always either avoided puzzles or tried to solve them. He had no use for things left dangling and unfinished.

Was it a child's school lesson carefully copied out of a poetry book for class? The handwriting said a lot. Although there were places where the writer crossed out words, the writing showed control with a precise, tight script.

No, it wasn't the work of a child. A dippy teenager with a large case of puppy love, probably. It had to be a female. No man or boy he knew would write sappy stuff like this.

The paper was crisp but not curled tight along the edges as paper got after a while from exposure to the sun and wind. It hadn't been around long, that was for sure. It wouldn't hurt to ride to the northern section of the mesa later this week, check out that pile of tumbleweeds where he noticed bits of paper among them. Might give a clue as to who wrote the puzzling bit of poetry. The constant wind blew so hard that whoever put the paper in the tumbleweed could live in the next county.

Matt had no close neighbors. His ranch covered miles, not acres.

He grinned. Maybe he wouldn't tell off the lovesick teenager even if he caught the litterer. The notes would disintegrate into dust eventually, anyway, with no harm done.

The image of the notes turning to dust made him restless. He might miss something by not reading the next one, as if the ones already gone contained words he needed to know. He would come back tomorrow for the strays. The papers would still be here, Matt thought as he reined his horse toward home.

CHAPTER 2

Casey stood on the porch of the cabin, looking out toward the ridge. Something about the rim of mountains fascinated her. Minute by minute the colors changed over the summits depending on how the sun or clouds moved across them. The tree line stopped half way up the highest peak and among rocks in shaded areas, she was sure she saw snow. She wondered what secrets the mysterious looking behemoths held.

"Hey, Mom. Wouldn't it be great to have a horse?"

She turned to her son, perched on the rail with his skinny legs dangling over the edge, and fought an overwhelming urge to put a steadying hand on his shoulder. From the boy's frown, she sensed that would have been the wrong move. She needed to learn to let him make choices, to gain self-confidence. That was hard when she wanted to keep him safe from harm. She moved closer, hands poised near the railing. "A horse? You're kidding! I thought you didn't like horses."

Jake laughed, accompanied by a coughing spell. She waited patiently until it was over. This time the fit passed more quickly than usual. A good sign.

"I know they eat hay and apples. I saw a movie where this kid gave a horse an apple."

"I think I remember that one," she said.

Jake's answer was to continue dangling his legs over the porch rail. Casey reached out to put her hand on him.

He slid his leg away from her touch, his forehead tucked in little tight creases. "Aw, Mom. I'm not gonna fall." He slipped off the railing and jumped up and down on the step to show her he wasn't afraid.

She changed the subject, moving to the lowest step and sitting down. "Let's go on a picnic. It's not far to the bottom of the canyon. I saw a nice cottonwood tree by a creek down there. We could eat and nap. I'll read to you," she promised.

"Oh boy!" He jumped off the top step, landing in a heap against her, knocking the breath out of her for a moment. He nuzzled his head into her neck briefly, as he used to do when he was a baby.

His father had never tolerated kisses or any other kind of sentimental display from Jake. Only handshakes and occasional manly hugs were acceptable, as if he feared supporting what he saw as the boy's weakness.

"Mom! Look! I saw a deer down there in the woods."

Jake's voice interrupted her thoughts and she was grateful. They had to put their past aside. Her son was the only good to come from those years.

"I see it. Wait a minute and let it go away and then we're ready to go, too."

When the deer wandered off, Casey rose and they walked up the porch steps, hand in hand. In the kitchen, she sliced some ham and made sandwiches, then prepared a thermos of coffee for her and a jar of lemonade for him.

"Don't forget the chocolate chip cookies," he reminded her.

"Hey, I'm trying to keep it light. Your mom's not a pack mule." She threw in the latest paperback mystery she had been reading to him, something to do with cats and a detective. She'd have to remember, when she wrote her books, not to write down to children. Not all children were as advanced as Jake, but he enjoyed children's books too.

"I like you dressed like that," he said, cocking his head sideways.

"You mean jeans and this ratty old shirt?" Did Jake know she'd made off with his dad's good luck golfing shirt? Probably. Jake knew a lot of things he didn't let on. Casey grinned, the sun brighter for thinking of Richard's discomfort. It gave her a smug lilt of satisfaction, thinking of him hitting only bogies. She remembered how her fit of temper had made her stuff the shirt in the suitcase. Stuffed shirt, how appropriate!

"Yeah, back home you always wore dresses with high heels and your hair..." He gestured with his hands to signify her hair tied back against her neck.

"Hey, this suits me fine." She touched her fingers to the hair flying around her shoulders, free and uncontrolled in the dry, static air, with twisted curls that lay around her face. "Come on, kiddo, grab that cover from the foot of the bed and let's get going."

Casey felt her shirt pocket to check for Jake's extra inhaler. Sometimes he forgot to keep his handy. "Wait a minute. I'd better give you an allergy pill. We don't know what kind of vegetation we'll find by the creek."

"Do I have to?" His grin, coupled with an expression of calm acceptance, made her smile. She went inside to get the pill and a glass of water. When he was done, they set off down the canyon trail. At first, the path was barely discernible, littered with small stones and rocks. As they progressed downward, the shade from the huge pines and firs caused moss to grow among the rocks, making the way slippery when they crushed the vegetation beneath their shoes.

"Look at the bluebirds, Jake. And there's a cardinal. They must have nests way up there." She pointed to the tops where the sun just peeked through. Small flowers of every color imaginable littered the wayside, mixing with the wild shrubs and grasses.

Casey carried the lunch in her back pack with the rolled blanket tucked under one arm, using the other hand to hold on to Jake as they hiked down the steep path. At first, he pulled away, wanting to dart forward on his own.

"Jake, hold on to my hand." She used her firm, no-nonsense voice, which allowed no room for debate.

"Okay. Guess you could use some help, since you're carrying everything."

"Right you are. You don't want your mom rolling into a spit ball and beating you down to the bottom, do you?"

He laughed and held on to her hand.

By the time they had hiked to the floor of the small canyon, the afternoon sun had changed sides. The shade from the huge cottonwood tree spread over the glen. The abrupt change from walking in mostly sunshine to coming into the dappled shade made goosebumps rise on her arms and the back of her neck. She spread the blanket underneath the tree and insisted they rest, although Jake wanted to explore. They lay listening to the stream rippling through the rocks close by.

"Tired?" Sometimes the allergy pills made him sleep for a short time. But they had walked slowly, stopping to rest often.

"Nah. Hungry and thirsty."

"Great. If you have much more of an appetite, I'll have to widen our doorways. They're kind of narrow."

When they finished eating, they both lay back to stare at the leafy canopy overhead. The wind blew softly, while the sun sifted down between the thick leaves like a golden mist.

"Want me to read?"

Jake shook his head. "I like to listen to the frogs. Sometimes they say things."

"Real words, like we do?" she asked.

Another shake and this time a gleam of mischief in his eyes. "That's silly, course not, but I think they understand each other."

"I bet they do." She smiled and closed her eyes, letting the moving shadows play on her eyelids. An odd rustling noise woke her. She didn't know how long she had been asleep, but she awoke with a sense of someone watching. She sat up, rubbing her eyes and staring into the unsmiling face of a man on huge, black and gray speckled horse. For a moment, she credited her imagination. Had she been dreaming? He seemed too big to be real. No, this man's sudden appearance was not a part of her imagination. She couldn't have dreamed up anyone like him.

She looked toward Jake who still slept, curled in a ball, hands clasped beneath his cheek. Nothing would wake him until he was finished sleeping. Casey leaped to her feet, hands on hips, ready to do battle. With a mouth lined in cotton, she had a hard time swallowing. Her pulse raced, and the vein in her neck throbbed.

The man sat easily on the horse. With his dark green wool shirt tucked in the waistband of tight, well-worn jeans and boots firmly placed in the saddle stirrups, he could have stepped from the pages of a western novel.

Observing the stranger's impassive, stony visage, she worried about Jake. Would he wake up at the wrong time? She wondered what to use for a weapon if she had to.

The man swept off his hat, gesturing with it toward the canyon walls. "This is Tyree land. What are you doing here?" Coming from his wide chest, his voice was deep. Definitely unfriendly.

"It's not fenced. I didn't see any posted signs," she retorted.

"No need to post signs. Strangers never come this way." His voice dipped to a low, hoarse whisper, when he apparently noticed the sleeping boy.

"Are you Matthew Tyree?" Nothing his mother had said prepared her for the man in front of her.

He nodded, not speaking.

Oh boy, a man of few words—John Wayne type, she would bet. She returned his scrutiny. Without the hat, he wasn't quite as formidable as he had seemed. His hair was thick and dark, with a touch of silver nudging over the tops of his ears. His face was tanned a warm brown. The hard planes of his cheekbones and the slight hawkishness of his nose were at odds with the smile lines around his eyes. Those eyes, coffee brown, held her transfixed so that she could not have turned away even if she wanted to.

He finally moved. Amidst the creaking of leather, he gracefully slung a long leg across the horse's rear to dismount.

"You know who I am," he said. "Who're you?"

"Catherine Nichols. That's my son, Jake."

He seemed to wait for her to explain their presence, but stubbornly, she refused to speak out.

"Mind if I sit a spell?"

"It's your land," she reminded him.

His wide mouth spread in a grin that showed white teeth. "I guess I had that coming. You still didn't say how you came to be on my land."

Casey paced in front of him while he seemed perfectly at home sitting on a large rock. Just what she needed, another take-over male. "This is so awkward. Didn't your mother tell you to expect us?"

He smacked his forehead with his palm. "You're C. J. Nichols? She left out the part about a woman answering that damned ad. Her idea, by the way."

Casey stopped pacing to stare at him. "Don't you need a groundskeeper?" Whatever that was. "Your mother said I should come. She did mention you were a bit—reclusive—but surely you don't think I just dropped in here without permission from someone."

To his credit, he looked confused but the annoyed tone stayed in his voice. "Damn it, I don't like surprises and I told her—"

She cut him off, before he could work up a head of steam, and motioned toward the blanket. "Come, sit here. That rock has to be cold and hard. There's some coffee in the thermos and maybe you'd like a chocolate chip cookie. They're Jake's favorite."

He ignored her attempt at appeasement. "I need someone to pick up at the stables and corral and trim the bushes along the side of the house. You don't look like you've ever worked outside." His voice was firm and unyielding while his frown and the look he raked over her were formidable. If she hadn't had to deal with Richard's temper through the years, she might have tucked tail and given up.

"I was under the impression that your parents owned the ranch. Your mother didn't seem to think it illogical that

I could do this job." So there, Mr. Smarty. It came as a surprise that being able to talk back to a stranger was much easier than arguing with Richard and a lot more satisfying.

"They do own the ranch, but that's going to change." He mouthed the words as if he had something sour on the end of his tongue. "I don't think my dad agrees one hundred percent."

"Why not?"

"A rancher is what a man is, not just what he does. You never quit ranching as long as you have property."

He was so sure of himself. That did not set well with Casey. She didn't need another arrogant male in her life. Like the tumbleweed, she and Jake should probably be moving along. Still, she could use that bonus he offered and she needed somewhere for them to stay hidden for a while.

But it didn't look like he was going to make it easy.

CHAPTER 3

He folded his legs to sit. As she knelt to pour the coffee, she couldn't help noticing even though he had long legs, he did everything gracefully.

Their hands touched, barely, when she gave the cup to him, but that touch sent jagged lightning through her fingers so she almost dropped the mug. It didn't help her composure when his strong fingers tightened on hers to hold them steady. Before he let go, he turned one of her palms up to peer into it.

"Are you a palm reader?" She asked, not pulling her hand away.

He looked up at her with an almost-grin. "Nope, but I can see from yours that you've never done any manual labor in your life." He dropped her hand and carefully selected the largest cookie.

Oh lordy, he would think she was a nut case. Then again, maybe he hadn't noticed anything odd in her hand trembling.

"That doesn't mean I can't do manual labor. The least you can do is give me a chance. What have you got to lose?"

Matthew frowned and ignored her question, asking one of his own. "How'd you find this place?"

"We came down the trail from the cabin. We've been staying there almost two weeks waiting for you to show up. I feel like a leech staying somewhere and not paying my way."

The muscles in his chiseled jaw worked, but his sooty eyelashes hid his expression. "You can stay until you find someplace to go. Parker's only sixty miles from here."

She considered telling him to climb back up on his horse and ride off, but that wouldn't have been too swift since this was his land. "I think it's only fair that you let me prove my worth as a groundskeeper. I promised your mother I'd stay until you came back."

"And you always keep your promises?"

"I try to. Surely seeing me a couple of times a day for a few months shouldn't interfere with your life." Casey didn't like defending her position, but this was a perfect place to hide away from Richard and his parents until she could get her act together.

His mouth turned down into a stubborn line. He shook his head. "I don't need a—I don't want—"

"I didn't know men like you still existed. Are you aware of women having the right to vote now? I can do the job or I wouldn't have applied for it."

For a long while he didn't speak. Casey thought her idea of getting away from it all would be for nothing. She would not beg to be allowed to stay where they weren't wanted.

"We could try it, I reckon. Especially since you promised." Matthew munched on another cookie absentmindedly as if he hadn't noticed picking it up out of the zipped bag.

"If you're at all curious, Jake and I needed somewhere to live for a while. That's one reason why we're here."

Matthew's brows drew into a frown. "I said Parker's not far."

"Hey, lighten up. I won't get in your way. I'll be almost invisible. Just point me to the stables and tell me what you want done. I don't have to haul horse sh—manure in a bag over my shoulder, do I? I'm sure you have a wheelbarrow."

Was that a chuckle or did he burp from the cookie and coffee? "This is nowhere for a kid to be. Winter's coming on." He gestured toward the sleeping boy, the second time he had acknowledged him.

The matter-of-factness of his words kept them from hurting, but his tone was resolute.

Matthew Tyree was obviously a close-minded domineering type, used to controlling everyone in his domain, including the family dog. She would never accept bossing from anyone ever again. If she ever did allow a man into her life, she knew exactly what she wanted. He must be a sensitive, caring, and responsive man she could talk to. A man with a sense of humor as off-the-wall as hers, one who would share his thoughts and feelings. Most important, he had to be romantic. This man definitely did not think romantic thoughts, in spite of looking like a dashing movie cowboy.

"We can leave, then, if you insist. I just need a few days to get organized and get Jake used to the idea." She wouldn't be as successful hiding out in a town like Parker. In those little places, everyone knew everyone else's business probably.

"Don't get your lasso on so tight. I merely made an observation."

The impact of that calm, steady gaze riveted on her face unsettled her.

The frogs began croaking loudly as if on a signal. The air resounded with their noise near the creek, echoing back and forth over the water.

"Jake claims frogs can talk," Casey said.

"They might. Just because we can't hear or understand a creature doesn't mean it's not communicating."

She thought about his words, which seemed quite revealing for someone on the taciturn side, and filed his comment away in her memory.

The air had cooled, making her realize the sun would soon set. They had better pack up and leave. Still, she didn't want to awaken Jake while this man was here. She rose to her knees and he got to his feet to help her up.

Her heart lurched to see him standing so near. When she looked up into his face, the ruggedness of his countenance did crazy things to her heartbeats. She felt his breath on the top of her head, stirring her hair. It was pure physical attraction, she told herself. He represented everything in a man she didn't want.

His gaze touched her face, lingered on her mouth.

She inched away to put some distance between them. "I need to wake my son now. It'll be dark soon. You can leave us here, we'll be fine."

"I'll wait. Give him a ride." He nodded toward his horse that had been patiently nipping grass along the edge of the water.

Casey stared at the animal, which, at this point loomed as large as an elephant. "On that horse?" She gasped and then got hold of herself." You will do no such thing. Jake doesn't care for horses, he—"

"All kids like horses, bar none."

"Here." She handed him the bag of cookies. "I can bake more for Jake. It will startle him to see a stranger when he wakes up."

Matthew accepted the cookies as gracefully as her words would allow, but she could tell her abrupt dismissal offended him.

"You remind me of a mama quail. Gets her back up when anything comes near her nest, flits around trying to distract and surrenders herself if she has to. To protect her young."

She smiled, surprised at his perception, that he would understand part of where she was coming from, protecting Jake. "I don't know about quail. I may be like that. Mothers are, aren't they?"

Jake stirred. She knelt at his side, shaking him gently. "Wake up sleepy head. We have company."

He stretched, awake in an instant, his eyes wide with excitement and not a sign of fear as he studied the towering man.

She was so proud of him.

Matthew knelt on one knee and took off his hat. "I'm Matthew Tyree. You can call me Matt."

Jake extended his hand. "I'm Richard Jacob Nichols. You can call me Jake."

Casey noticed that Matthew also had difficulty keeping a straight face at Jake's grown-up voice.

"Like horses?"

The boy looked at the horse, his eyes lit up. "Wow. He's big! I think I like pictures of horses better. He's a funny color with those gray spots and streaks. Is he old?"

"No, he's not old. He's called a *steel dust*. How about me setting you up there for a second?"

"No!" Casey rushed behind Jake to put both hands on his shoulders.

He jerked away from her and ran toward the horse with arms waving in the air. The horse, startled, took off running along the shore and cut through the woods with Jake running behind.

"Now see what you've done?" Casey's voice rose to near-hysteria and she ran after the horse and boy. Above the sound of her panting, she heard a sharp whistle from Matt.

Immediately the sound of crashing brush passed by her and Jake, heading in Matt's direction. They turned and went back to the clearing. The horse was there, trembling but standing still.

Casey and Jake were both out of breath and had pieces of brush and leaves in their hair.

"Son, never run up to any critter in a hurry. They don't understand you're just excited to meet them," Matt said.

"You could have called the horse back before he ran a mile through the woods," Casey accused.

A grin tugged at the corner of his mouth. "Could have."

She felt awkward and silly and wanted to smack him one. This didn't look too well for her job as a groundskeeper, but her first thought was for Jake. He bent over gasping for air. She knelt in front of him and pulled out his puffer from his jacket pocket. "Here. This will help."

Jake took several puffs until he finally got his breath under control.

"You okay?" Matt asked.

Jake nodded, and Casey could tell he was ashamed of his asthma spell.

"That was a pretty good run. Bet you're ready for a ride." he asked Jake.

"I said no!"

"Mom." Jake swerved to brush off her hands. "It won't hurt. I *want* to sit up there."

Matt rubbed his fingers along the rim of his hat before he clamped it back on his head. "It won't harm Jake to sit up there a minute. I wouldn't let him if I thought there was any danger to it."

"Well, I guess it can't hurt." He had already undermined her authority. Now he was making her look witchy in front of her son. Did she attract bossy men? Horrible thought.

Matt adjusted the stirrups as high as they would go.

Smiling from ear to ear, Jake held up his arms for a lift.

"We won't do it that way. We'll do it the big boy's way. Make your legs stiff so they won't bend." He laced his fingers together and nodded for Jake to step up. Then Matt raised him upward and put Jake's left foot in the stirrup. Jake flung his right leg over the horse's broad back and eased up onto the saddle.

"There, see how easy that was?" Matt turned to Casey standing close enough to touch the stirrups. "The boy is light—like a piece of dandelion fluff in my hands."

Did he think she was underfeeding Jake?

"Don't be scared, Mom." Jake held tight to the saddle horn with one hand and flung the other in a dramatic flair. "I feel like I got that Superman cape on. Remember the one you made me when I was a little kid? I can see everything. I'm a giant. I can touch the tree tops."

"You can get off now. You're much too heavy for this poor skinny nag." Matt held out his hands to help Jake down.

Jake laughed with delight at the joke and shook his head. "I can do it."

They watched Jake lift his leg over the gelding's wide rump and reach for the ground with the toes of his tennis shoes. Matt took his leg, which Jake remembered to stiffen as he had before.

On the ground, the boy stretched his skinny arms upward as far as they would go, trying to reach around the long neck of the horse. "Thank you, horse," he whispered. "I really like you."

Casey was surprised when Matt looked away for a moment, as if the boy's connection with the horse moved him. Probably her imagination.

"Hey! That was neat! What's his name?" Jake giggled when the horse pushed his nose through his hair, snuffling and smelling. Casey rushed forward to grab him away.

Matt blocked her. "He likes you. That's just his way of saying you're okay."

Jake stood still, allowing the horse to nuzzle his head, until his uneasy giggles burst into wild laughter. He ended up coughing a bit, but Casey held back and the spasm of coughing soon passed as they laughed with him.

"What *is* his name?" Casey asked when the moment of hilarity passed.

"Dam—darned if I know. The last dog I named died from a rattlesnake bite, so don't see any reason to name anything else."

"His name's Smokey," Jake decided. "Is that okay?"

"Sure thing. Looks like a cloud of smoke, doesn't he?"

"I'll draw a picture of him to put inside the—"

"We have to go now," Casey interrupted, cutting Jake off in mid-sentence. "I'm sure Mr. Tyree has things he should be doing and we have to get up that trail before dark. And don't ask, you are *not* riding on that horse!"

Matt swung up into the saddle in a smooth, fluid movement. "Some other time, maybe." He spoke directly to Jake. "I won't be going out on the range again for a spell. We'll talk about your leaving. I haven't brought in the horses from the range anyway." He touched a finger to the brim of his hat in a salute and headed the horse through the trees.

"I liked him, Mom." Jake was practically jumping up and down with excitement.

That worried her, down here alone with no one to help if he should get into one of his more serious spells. "Why don't you calm down a little and take a swig of juice and then we'll pack our stuff and head up the trail. I sure don't want to be out here after dark." She was glad Jake didn't ask if *she* liked Matthew Tyree. She never lied to Jake, but she didn't want to confess the man brought out the biggest chip on her shoulder. And it didn't seem as if he was going to let them stay. When were they ever going to get a break?

That night, Casey lay awake, tossing and turning, throwing off the covers and then retrieving them from the floor, unable to banish Matthew Tyree from her thoughts. He was the sexiest man she had ever seen outside an ad in a magazine. The muscles in his upper arms looked taut and hard even through the long sleeved shirt he wore. She remembered trying not to stare at his hands, so strong and browned from the sun.

It was enough to keep her awake many nights if she did not get a grip on her reaction. She forced herself think of his personality, so full of certainty and disciplined, as if he knew just what he wanted from life and expected it to be there for him. She was strong enough now she didn't need a man like that in her life. Hadn't she had enough drama when she left Richard?

Richard. Forget Richard, she scolded herself. That life was past, time to discard it. Right then she made a vow to wipe her ex from her mind and heart. She vowed not to speak his name in her mind again. He must have cared for her at the beginning of their marriage, but her pregnancy changed everything. He often told her how cow-like she was and let her know in so many ways how ugly he thought she'd become. The only time he ever hit her was when she carried Jake.

Richard had undermined her self-esteem in so many ways during their marriage. He'd insisted she stop writing. It was a passion that did not include him, and he couldn't abide having her ignore him when she felt in the mood to write. Then there was Mr. Peterson, the tutor. He made her feel Jake's age and no telling how he made Jake feel. The boy seldom talked about him. But Richard had to have someone with authority teaching Jake because he said she was too soft and had no backbone when it came to discipline.

That had to be one of the most hurtful things he had ever laid on her doorstep. She was not going to let him do it to her any more.

Matt had gone back to the line shack one more time to get the last bunch of strays. He lifted his third cup of morning coffee to his lips and then set it back down on the rickety table with a resounding slam. Time to get home. Camping out in line shacks had lost its appeal. Thirty-five was too old to be doing this. Yet, he valued his privacy and didn't want help except for round up and branding. For sure, he didn't want some fluffy bit of a woman with a kid banging on his door every day. Wait until he saw his mother again, he would finally lay the law down.

"Hellfire!" He wiped futilely at the widening pool of spilled coffee that ran toward the small pile of crumpled notes he had retrieved from the tumbleweeds.

Where did the notes come from? Who wrote them? His hand played with the papers, touching the last one, parts of which he still remembered. A great deal of his anger was directed inward, he realized. The poems touched something buried deep within, causing him to respond to emotions he never wanted to feel again.

Instead of scanning the horizon for strays, he found himself studying the terrain, hoping for a glimpse of white paper entangled in the brush. It unsettled him, as a man who valued his routine, to have the mystery of where he might find the next note. He never tolerated uncertainty well. That caused some of the annoyance with the randomly scattered papers, he told himself. The reality slowly emerged into his thoughts. His life must be pathetically empty to make such a deal out of a few poems written by what was likely some lovesick teenager.

It had been nearly eight years since he lost everything in the accident. Why couldn't he let the guilt and frustration go? Well, hell, this was not getting him anywhere. He slammed out of the shack and headed for the corral. He was over the urge to get away from the house. He needed to get back to familiar surroundings. It was those infernal notes he kept finding, stuck in the bellies of the tumbleweeds that made him restless. If it took riding over the entire countryside, he was going to discover who was writing them.

And why.

CHAPTER 4

Matt rode toward the cabin on the side of the hill. He had to see the woman and get it over with. He didn't want her and her boy here. She was over-protective and irritating, and he was sure she would not stay past the first week of work, but why chance it?

He supposed having another female on the ranch just changed things, and he didn't like change. Odd how, after so long, the edges on his memories of Dorothy were beginning to fuzz over, like the black stuff on an old mirror. Would the dark shadows gradually creep into the center, blocking each remembrance?

Just as he topped the rise on the trail leading to the cabin, he paused to watch the boy insert a paper into a tumbleweed and the woman lift it in her arms to send it off into the wind. He had the answer to the mystery of the notes. Why wasn't he surprised? He tilted his hat back to watch the tumbleweed bounce down the mountainside, sailing in the direction of the box canyon where many of them had collected. For brief moment he considered whether gathering the notes he had collected so far was like eavesdropping. But didn't sending them off into space mean it was not important who read them?

He waited for the two to turn away before kneeing the horse closer. It was obviously their secret, and he respected that.

"Hello, anyone home?" He called on his way up, trying not to startle them. *Turn around and leave, don't get involved,* a voice told him.

Casey smiled in greeting. She held her son's hand, but he pulled away when he saw Matt.

"Mom! The horse! It's Smokey!" Jake squealed and started down the steps.

"Wait, take it easy," she called after him, but he ran forward.

Her lips parted, and her mouth worked with words she didn't say, as if she started to shout more cautions to the boy but stopped at the last minute.

"Mornin', Jake. Remember us?" Matt swung his leg off the horse.

"Sure do." Jake offered his small hand, which Matt carefully engulfed in his big one. The boy's chest puffed visibly, and he shot a lopsided grin at his mother. *See, I'm shaking hands with a real cowboy. Just like a man.*

It was as easy to know what Jake was thinking as if he spoke out loud.

Without warning, his eyes widened and his face turned pale. He began wheezing, gasping for air. Casey flew down the steps, barely touching them, to reach her son.

Matt knelt to put his hands on Jake's shoulders. He shook his head to stop Casey's headlong flight. "Son, take it easy. Breathe in and out, come on, that's a big boy. Easy does it. Relax, real slow like."

Miraculously, Jake took a deep breath and the hiccoughing breaths subsided.

Matt saw tears in Casey's eyes when he pushed Jake gently toward her.

"How'd you manage that?" she asked.

He shrugged. "Common sense. It might not work every time, but I noticed he seemed to be building to a peak. He got a little more excited than was good for him, I guess."

Jake's cheeks turned from pale to red, and he turned his face away.

Matt touched him on the shoulder to get his attention. "Hey, kid, everyone has a problem or two. No reason to get bent out of shape about it. I wake up some mornings so stiff, I have to crawl out of bed. That's from riding in the saddle all day."

"Really?" Jake turned back to look at Matt, his movements still jerky and tentative, as if ready to retreat at any moment.

"Say, I bet you've spent a lot of hours in the sun since you came here," Matt said.

"I guess."

"You're getting a real tan. Soon you'll be all weather-beaten like a regular cowboy."

Jake giggled. "For sure? Mom, did you hear? I'm getting a tan. I'll look 'xactly like a cowboy."

Casey laughed. "I heard. You are definitely getting a tan. It's good of Mr. Tyree to notice and point it out to you."

Her lips were tight, and she looked out of sorts. Could it be she was a little jealous of him getting some of Jake's attention and maybe felt guilty about it? The boy was staring up at him with hero-worship bright in his eyes, which wasn't hard to take, even if he hardly deserved it.

"Can I pet Smokey?" Jake asked.

"I don't see why not, but better check with your mom first." He was already holding Jake's open palm against the horse's velvety nose. She had to know he would never chance allowing harm to come to the boy.

"How about a cup of coffee and a piece of pie?"

Matthew felt his mouth splitting in a smile a mile wide. What could it hurt? It might make it harder to tell her she had to go, but eventually there would be an opening. "Just give me a minute to take the saddle off Smokey. We came in from the line shack this morning, and he needs a roll in the grass."

There wasn't much grass around, just a patch or two of green weeds all grown together. He looked toward the side of the cottage and then turned back quickly so they wouldn't notice that he had found their cache of tumbleweeds tucked close between the old wooden shed and the cabin.

♞

"Can I stay and watch him?" Jake asked

"Some other time," Casey said. "I need a word with you, in private." She marched him up the stairs while Matt took care of his horse.

She felt Matt's eyes on her as they walked up the steps. How good that was of him to fib to her son about his health to put them on even terms. Judging from that magnificent frame and those wiry muscles showing underneath his rolled-up sleeves, he probably never had a sick day in his life.

"I apologize for dragging you away like that," she said to Jake when they were out of earshot. "I just want to be sure you remember our conversation about keeping our tumblewords a secret." She hadn't missed the hero-worship in her son's eyes, and that troubled her. She had to admit to feeling a little jealousy. No, actually a lot of jealousy. She was not ready to share him with anyone. But that wasn't it entirely. She had poured too much of her raw feelings into her poems in the tumbleweed, showing needs that she didn't want anyone to know about. Hadn't even wanted to admit to herself.

If he should discover them, this sensible, unromantic man was sure to find her outpourings childish and nonsensical to his pragmatic way of thinking. That would greatly diminish her joy of expressing herself.

"I remember, I really do," Jake told her.

"Good, then I'm going to run a comb through this messy hair and I'll be right out."

She went into the bedroom. Lordy, he couldn't be impressed by this mop of unruly, static-filled bunch of curly hair, she thought, not really wanting to look into the mirror but unable not to. It made her smile, looking at herself without a barrette to hold the mass in place or at least force it up off her neck in a French twist. She finished brushing as best she could. Then she stood, watching through the partly opened doorway when Matt entered the main room of the cabin, wanting to see his reaction. Inside the house, Matt's head almost touched the ceiling. He held his worn Stetson in his hand.

Whatever belonged to her, she found room to fit into the car when they left Phoenix. Her possessions changed things enough so the cabin didn't look like it did before. The bright pillows on the couch and in front of the fireplace reflected color against the shiny hardwood floor. She'd put down hand woven area rugs that her mother had made and placed glass vases filled with brightly colored silk flowers on the fireplace mantle and in the middle of the maple kitchen table.

She opened the door and pointed toward the big, easy chair. "Sit, please." She knew her tone had an edge, but she wasn't sure how comfortable she felt with this man's presence filling up their tiny cabin. She watched him take in the decorated room.

"Looks nice," he commented, emitting a sigh when he sat down in the well-broken-in chair. He leaned back while Jake pulled up an ottoman to put his booted feet on.

"Thanks, Son. That's good."

Casey brought him a slice of pie and set it on the end table in front of him. She and Jake took smaller pieces and sat on the couch. The homey aroma of coffee spread around the room.

"Say, I could get used to this kind of treatment," Matt said.

"Me too," Jake piped up, his mouth full of pie.

They laughed at him and Jake accepted it good-naturedly.

"It's quiet out here," Matt said.

"Yes, it is. But Jake and I have lots of things to interest us."

"City people have no business being here for any length of time. Gets mighty lonesome."

Casey hoped he would find it a little hard to order them to leave while he was holding a cup of her coffee and eating her pie. She at least wanted to delay the inevitable.

She wrinkled her nose, and took a deep breath, about to say something sarcastic and realizing how inappropriate that was. Sure, there were lonely moments, but she had been a lot lonelier inside her marriage than she was outside it.

Silence surrounded them except for the sound of their chewing. "I haven't progressed as far as thinking of winter. Too busy trying to live one day at a time. We're content, city people or not. I doubt you can generalize, since we are not all made the same. I enjoy writing, and Jake likes to draw. I showed him how to work with pastels."

Her father, what little she remembered of him, was artistic and left many paintings and drawings behind. Jake was especially adept at drawing animals, probably because he had always wanted a pet. It was one thing she didn't dare give him, not with all his allergies.

"That's good, drawing's good," Matt said. His casual glance around the house said there was little to do in the way of housekeeping. "What keeps you busy?"

"I write." Had she said too much? Had he seen the notes in the tumbleweeds? She didn't think so. "I'm just finishing a children's book. Jake's offered to illustrate it for me."

"Sounds like a family project."

Jake pretended not to listen but Casey knew better.

Particularly when he squared his shoulders and said, "Yeah, family. We're a family." His thin voice came out strident, daring Matt to challenge him.

Such a serious kid, and yet he shared her kind of humor, her sense of fun. He just tucked it away temporarily. He brought it out increasingly with time. Maybe being sick so much had neutralized a lot of humor that would return as he grew healthier.

Their guest didn't seem over-endowed with a sense of humor, although nature had pretty well covered every other aspect. Good thing neither she or Matthew had any inclination for a flirtation, because under normal circumstances, his striking good looks and the larger-than-life ruggedness of his bone-hard physique might have tempted her. For sure these wayward thoughts made her realize how vulnerable she still was.

"You asked me questions, now it's my turn," she said. He had been observing her with such speculation in his eyes, she had the uneasy feeling he knew her thoughts. A daft idea. She poured him another cup of coffee. "What do *you* do all day?"

He grinned, apparently not taking offense at her comeback. "When you live on a ranch, there's no end to it. I stay busy rounding up strays. Found cougar tacks on the ridge last month. Need to keep watch. I work on the buildings or they would all be falling down around our ears, everything's so old around here. Something's always falling apart."

"You don't have anyone to help you?" Casey tried to ignore the wide-eyed fascination on Jake's face, probably at Matt's mention of the cougar.

"Some help. Not as much as we've had in the past. A few of the boys stay in the bunkhouse, cook their own meals, live out in the line shacks during spring roundup. Paco and Carmela live here."

"Do they live on the ranch permanently?"

He nodded. "When I was a kid, we kept a bunkhouse full of cowboys. But with intelligent marketing practices a rancher can make as much on a lot less cattle."

"Sounds complicated."

"It's not. Just takes planning. I haven't been able to convince Pop to change from his old way of doing things yet. Paco helps a lot, even if he is getting on in years. He's lived here since they poured foundations on the place. Pop swears he came up whole from the first slab of cement. No one seems to remember how he came to be here."

She liked the way he explained things. Even though he was a man of few words, he didn't seem stingy with using them once he got started. "What about Carmela?"

"Paco left once, or so the story goes. Disappeared for a week, took a trip across the border and brought Carmela back as his wife."

Casey smiled at Jake, knowing he was eating this up, remembering every detail to talk about later. "What does Paco look like?"

"He's skinny and quiet, with a kind of old-fashioned dignity. His mustache takes up half of his face, like in the pictures of Pancho Villa. Dorothy used to tease him, said they were probably *primos*, cousins. He got a kick out of that. Carmela is the opposite. She's as round as she is tall and talks all the time, even when no one's listening."

"Do you visit your parents in town? Take trips with them?"

"Great balls of fire, woman, you sure are full of questions. I'm about to run out of answers." He hit his hat against his leg, which she noticed he did sometimes when he didn't know how to reply.

He made a short, derisive noise like Jake might do when he was disgusted with something. "Why would I need to get away from here? My folks know they can come home anytime they want. Never saw the need for traveling around just for the sake of traveling."

"Does everything have to be a necessity? A lot of enjoyable things may not be practical but—"

"Nothing wrong with it. I'm not sitting in judgment. Let them golf or play tennis or go to the movies or dance, those just aren't *my* priorities."

"Okay, fair enough. Then what is? Your priority, I mean."

"The ranch. It has been my idea to make it pay again. Make it a working ranch like it used to be only with newer techniques. Pop maintains the days of small ranches are numbered, but with new procedures and improved stock, I don't think so." His dark eyes lit with banked excitement.

He was passionate about something, which was good. Had he said it all? Wasn't he going to elaborate? She had never been around a man who didn't enjoy talking on and on about himself. She imagined that was a man-thing.

"So, what about you?" Matt asked.

Casey thought for a moment. "At this point, it's hard to say. Get Jake well. I want him in school, rather than home schooled. He needs to be with other kids, but on an even basis. I'd like to finish a book and sell it so I can support us." *Find the love of my dreams someday*, she wanted to add.

"Mmm," was his only comment.

Casey watched her son, seeing him from Matt's perspective. His blond hair was lifeless, brittle like straw. His skinny body and pale skin coupled with the bruised color under his eyes made him resemble a wizened little old man.

Would he ever get well? She had to believe he would. The doctor she trusted said he would likely grow out of the allergies and asthma. But when?

She caught Matt watching Jake, but she couldn't read the look deep in his eyes. Was it sympathy? Casey hoped it wasn't pity.

"Jake, show Mr. Tyree some of your work, the stuff we're going to put in our book."

"Call me Matt. Mr. Tyree sounds silly when I'm sitting in your living room drinking your coffee," He said. "I'd like to see what you draw, son."

The boy hesitated and then slowly rose from his place on the couch. When he was nervous, he moved in jerky starts, as if the parts of his body didn't work together, and he stuttered. His father had been so impatient with the stuttering.

Jake brought the sketchbook from his bedroom and tentatively laid it in Matt's lap.

Matt opened it and looked through the pages, concentrating on what he saw. "Say, this is dam—darned good drawing, Jake."

His praise sounded sincere and Jake pushed out his chest, swelling with pride.

While Matt looked in the book, Casey watched him, knowing his attention was focused on Jake. This man filled a room. Lean and hard, with shoulders like a linebacker, the man had been baked to a smooth mahogany color by the elements. The curious idea of what color his skin would be underneath his jeans caused a blush to rise and redden her face.

"You okay, Mom?" Jake started toward her in alarm.

"I'm fine." She moved away, but not before catching Matt's obvious amusement. Great. She hoped she wasn't that transparent. The guy didn't miss much, probably because he stayed out searching the countryside for his darned stray cattle all of the time.

Matt touched Jake's head with his fingers—just the tips, as if he would pull away as soon as Jake noticed. "Both of you are light skinned. Redheads and blondes are more delicate. Our sun can be deceiving, it may look overcast but it's still shining down. You need to wear hats when you're outdoors."

"I figured that. I'm not an idiot." She took a deep sip of coffee, striving for control. He was telling them for their own good, but now that she was free of Richard, dominant bossiness had no place in her life anymore.

"Never said you were." Matt went back to Jake's drawings and peered closely at them. "I like what you've done. This roadrunner—what say, you move that leg back and the other one forward just a tad, stretch his neck up a bit to give the impression of movement. Those rascals are never still. I have always wondered what they do at night. Hop, hop, and hop from one foot to another all night long? Can you picture that? Can you see them open their right eye, hop on the left foot and then...get the idea?"

Jake got it. They looked on while he tried it out, imitating the movement and when they laughed at him, he rolled on the floor with wild giggles, holding his sides.

Casey knew he had formed a mental view of the bird doing what Matt described. She supposed there wasn't anything very wrong with her son's sense of humor. "Careful, you'll roll into the furniture." *You'll hurt yourself*, she almost said, but caught the words before they could escape. He could be touchy about her cautions, especially in front of people.

"He's okay, don't fret so."

"What do you know?" Her words came out sharper than she intended, but she couldn't turn away from the challenge. "I'll bet you never had a sick day in your life."

He shrugged. "Maybe. Maybe not. But the boy doesn't seem so sick. Let him be. That's what a boy likes, to just be."

Casey frowned, liking the part of what he said and trying not to take offense at what she considered his authoritative attitude. To change the subject, she said, "We're from Phoenix. Have you ever been there?" His boots were so rooted in the Colorado soil, she doubted it.

"Oh, I've ventured out of Colorado." He grinned at her challenge. "Pop and I made cattle selling and buying trips as far as New Mexico. In fact, I raced quarter horses in Texas a couple of seasons. I don't bother anymore since...I seldom even go into Center City, and that's only a three-hour drive. I have everything I need right here."

How lucky for you, she thought, without a trace of the sarcasm the words might have had if she'd spoken them. When Casey glanced in Jake's direction, he had curled up on the couch in a familiar position of sleep.

Matt noticed and smiled. "Is it nap time?"

"He can sleep at a drop of a hat. Anywhere."

Matt was not very skilled at whispering, not that anything could waken Jake until he was ready.

"There's something we need to discuss," he said. For once, he didn't seem so sure of himself.

"Let's go on the porch, Mr. Tyree."

"Call me Matt," he said again, following her outside.

When they moved out of the narrow door, Casey caught her heel on the rubber mat. She felt the warmth and hardness of Matt's wide chest as he pulled her close to keep her from falling. She twisted against him to hold her balance. Matt was so near, her body molded to his solid, muscular frame.

He bent his head and his mouth covered hers hungrily, his lips demanding and urgent. The kiss shook her violently from the top of her head to the bottom of her soles.

Her immediate instinct was to arch away from him, a feeling that left as quickly as it had come, replaced by a hunger that matched his. Matt's heart thudded against her breasts that were taut and sensitive from the pull of her shirt.

Pure pleasure shot through her body. Her lips parted to receive his probing tongue. His deep-throated groan brought her to her senses and with a flushed face, she pulled away and walked shakily to sit on the wooden swing.

Matt leaned against the rail, watching her. A vein in his neck throbbed, the only sign of his disturbance.

"I—I don't know what came over me," Casey hesitated, feeling foolish. He had instigated it, why was she apologizing? She willed her heart to stop racing. It was just a kiss for heaven's sake. Maybe the best kiss she'd ever had, she thought, though she hated to admit it.

He looked away, staring off into the distance. His tongue touched his lips as if still feeling her mouth against them. "I don't know either. What came over me, I mean."

"I thought you might be coming up here to tell us we have to leave." Never one to mince words, she wanted to find out what was on his mind.

"I did."

"You've got a funny way of showing it."

He looked embarrassed, rubbing his hat against his leg and looking away, toward the edge of the yard.

He appeared as shaken as she was. They needed space and a topic of mutual interest. Jake was a safe subject. "Jake developed asthma along with various allergies early in his life and so far he's been great since we came to the ranch."

"Doesn't sound too serious." Matt's voice still sounded husky with unexpressed desire and he couldn't seem to look her in the eye.

She wondered what would have happened if she hadn't pulled away from him. "Most of his problem was stress related. His father and I—we quarreled a lot. Oh, not around Jake if we could help it, but kids are smart. They sense things."

"Seems like I've read somewhere that kids gradually grow out of asthma."

"That's what Richard thought. He figured taking his son to doctors was babying him. The doctors said different." Her voice sounded brittle, and she knew was reacting to Matt's judgment of her ability to care for her son.

"Hey, don't get your feathers ruffled. You're right, I've no business butting in, but you did bring it up. "

"I apologize. I'm so used to defending him to his father and Mr. and Mrs. Nichols. As if they think it's my fault that Jake isn't healthy and out playing soccer or baseball. He has had pneumonia three times already, and I've lost count of his hospital stays for bronchitis. It's serious enough. Plus, he's scared when he can't catch his breath."

"That would scare anyone. Didn't you think it could be risky, bringing the boy up here alone?"

"Yes. But he wasn't getting any better back there. Each time he went into a coughing spell, I took him to the hospital. When Richard and I split, I decided that was a sign. There had to be a way to help Jake...something better for him. The doctors agreed living in the city wasn't helping."

"Your ex didn't mind you taking Jake far away?"

Now he was treading a little too close to the center of their problem. She had to keep Jake away from her in laws until she figured out how she would support the two of them. Richard could help. He had the money, but she didn't want him in their lives. If he tired of his latest conquest, he might come looking for them, too.

"I have full custody of Jake. If my ex had decided to fight it, he could have, since he had money on his side. His parents think they know what is best for their grandson, always have. It isn't a topic of discussion with them, and I have tried. They refuse any compromise, although I don't know what sort of middle ground we could agree on even if they didn't. A boy needs his mother. Maybe in later years, if he wants to visit them for a period of time, that would work."

She sighed. The valley sloped gracefully downward to the canyon far below, giving them a panoramic view framed by the porch. She drew her legs up beneath her and settled deeper into the comfortable swing. "It's beautiful here. I love to hear the wind sighing through the brush at night."

"You should hear it through the pines. I could take you up there on the ledge someday, but you won't be staying long enough for that." His voice took on a hard edge, and he turned away again.

He kept harping on their leaving but he didn't seem to actually say the words. Not her problem. Until he came right out and told her to go, she was staying put. "Why'd your parents decide to leave the ranch? Isn't that unusual?"

Matt's lips spread in a grin that lit his face and smoothed away the hardness of his high cheekbones. "I've a feeling they'll be back. When I brought Dorothy here to live on the ranch, Pop and I built another house for us a half-acre away from the main one. When the folks left a couple of years ago, I moved into their house. I offered to move back out, if and when I clean Dorothy's stuff out."

It was worse than she imagined. He hadn't even removed his late wife's belongings from their old home. He might have tried to move away from his memories, but they seemed to have followed him. Casey admired his loyalty, his dogged sense of commitment. Would someone remember her that way?

"I told them they were welcome to move in the main house with me," he continued. "With four bedrooms it's not like we'd be crowded."

"It'd be a lot of company for you."

"I'd like them to come back, but I don't *need* company."

It seemed insulting, the way he said he didn't need company with emphasis on need. As if she did. "We don't need to have people around us every minute either. We like our little isolated spot just fine. I enjoy the solitude." So there, Mr. Self-Sufficient.

"You've been here two weeks, you said. Have you started your car?" He pointed at her car parked behind the cabin.

"Where would I go? Parker? Or Center City?"

"Doesn't matter. One's sixty miles away, one is a hundred eighty. I meant, if you don't use your car or start it once in a while the battery will die on you."

"I didn't think of that. I stocked up on supplies, but I have to drive Jake in for checkups. I could start the car once a week, or check on our mail at the post office in Parker more often." They never received any mail, just the occasional letter from her aunt and the bank statement showing deposit of Richard's monthly support check.

Casey understood about car batteries, but she let it pass, glad the chip on her shoulder was gradually melting away like an ice cube in summer. "Where do you pick up your mail?"

"What mail? The folks take care of it. That gives them an excuse to come when they bring me income tax forms and property tax bills. That's about it."

Self-sufficiency was one thing, but Matthew Tyree seemed to be as rigid and unmoving as the mountains. Yet, his kiss said otherwise.

"There's a phone at the main house. You're welcome to use it—ah, anytime," he offered.

She was certain he'd almost said until you leave. Maybe he'd decided that would be a little over doing it.

"I do have a cell phone," she said.

"Uh, uh. No good here, too much interference from the mountains and woods."

"I suppose you have electricity in the main house?"

"They finally got a line coming up here. We never brought it down to this cabin though."

In a way, she liked that. No television, no radio, no distractions. It was nice to light candles or the old-fashioned kerosene lamps at night, it made the house cozy. Someone had stacked plenty of wood out back for the fireplace. Her main worry was not having a phone at night, for Jake.

"Does that mean we can stay here? At least a while? You can show me what to do."

At first, she thought he was not going to answer.

He looked down at his boots and then at her again. "I guess you could stay until fall if you needed to. But there's no need for the outside work, Paco will be back soon enough."

Casey walked forward, hesitating to come too close.

He noticed and grinned down at her. She was close enough to see the mischief deep in his dark eyes and smell the wood smoke on his clothing with the faint horse and leather smell, a good smell.

"Stop by when you're in the neighborhood," she said. "I usually bake something for Jake's sweet tooth. You two appear to have that same vice."

"You don't, that's for sure. You seem kind of delicate." He smiled but his eyes stayed serious. "You take care of yourself. For Jake."

The look that passed between them sent zings down to the soles of her feet and she smiled back at him, feeling giddy like a schoolgirl with her first valentine.

He turned away, but not before she saw his jaw tighten, his eyes grow remote.

"I doubt I'll be dropping by." He cleared his throat brusquely. "Got things to keep me busy. You know where I am if you or Jake need anything."

"Wait!" She moved forward to put her hand on his arm. "I came here to work. Your mother said it would be fine. I can't just camp out on your property for nothing. Can't I at least do some cleaning or cooking for you?"

"I don't want...I'll wait for Carmela. I'm used to her bossing me around and I can take care of myself just fine. Do it all the time when I'm out on the line shacks, no Carmela out there."

"Okay, I understand. Still, I will feel obligated. I don't want to be where I am not wanted. Can I pay you rent?"

Matt shook his head and clamped on his hat. "Nope. If you want any exchange, you might bring Jake up once in a while so I can show him the cattle and the rest of the ranch. That will give me a break. But not too often." He held out his hand. "Let's just call it a friendship deal, okay?"

Casey didn't like it, but what choice did she have? She placed her hand in his to shake, but he held it tightly within his and gazed deeply into her eyes for a long moment.

"Tell Jake *adios* for me."

She understood Matt was attracted to her and yet he didn't want to be. It was a concept that sent her silly heart fluttering up in her throat, and she held her hand in front so he wouldn't see it. Her self-esteem must be as low as Jake's if she needed the lift of this man's attention. That was all that it was, pure and simple, just a sexual attraction from both sides, with neither wanting it to happen.

Matt was rolled up in his past like a caterpillar inside a cozy cocoon. It would take a few carloads of dynamite to break him loose from Dorothy, and Casey had neither the time nor the energy. Besides, he certainly was not what she wanted in a serious relationship. He was taciturn and reserved, a closed mind. She desperately needed roses, champagne, and courting. It was just as well, she decided. Having a friend might have been a good thing, but judging from the shared sizzle between them, friendship was out of the question.

There was no room for anyone else in her or Jake's life, anyway. Not now, maybe not ever again for her.

CHAPTER 5

Casey worked hard putting her book together, sitting up long hours after Jake went to bed and getting up in the morning at first light. She wanted Richard gone from her life and didn't want to need the child support he insisted on giving her to banish any guilt he might have felt. Those payments could also be a ploy by him and his parents to track her down. He had been very possessive of her before she became pregnant. But he hadn't shown any violent streak until then. Maybe because things became out of his control—how she looked, how she appeared to his country club buddies.

She had earned a decent living for herself before she got married, so why couldn't she do it again. The children's books she wrote should be better now—with the knowledge having a son brought her.

She stood on the porch in the early morning light and thought of the tumbleweeds hidden away at the side of the cabin. They made her fingers *itch* to write something. The purple mountains in the distance surrounded her new home in a protective hug, but sometimes early in the morning she saw vestiges of what had to be snow on the tops of some of them. A restless feeling slipped over her enjoyment of the quiet setting, as she remembered the hardness of Matt's body against hers, the pulsing awareness of that sensuous mouth covering hers.

The little world she had created for herself and Jake had been sufficient before Matt came on the scene. Admittedly, she missed adult companionship. It wasn't that she craved it, but she would've enjoyed having another person to talk to and exchange ideas with. It certainly had nothing to do with broad shoulders and knife-edged cheekbones.

She went back in the house and sat at the table to write another poem for the tumbleweed. Then she had to pack for their trip into town tomorrow.

Matt chopped wood for the fireplace. It was good vigorous exercise and helped him work off some of his frustration. If Paco had been there, Matt could just imagine him standing at the corner of the house, scratching his gray head, a puzzled expression on his weather-beaten face. What was the big deal? Just because Matt hadn't chopped wood since bringing home a power saw, it would have been no reason for Paco to stare. But Paco wouldn't have seen it that way.

Matt shucked off his damp shirt, stopping a moment to enjoy the prickly sensation of the cool breeze against his skin. The ax in his hands swung downward, slicing deep into the log and sending chips flying in all directions. Working feverishly, he tried to banish the forbidden images that tormented him. Maybe if he exhausted himself, he'd finally be able to sleep tonight without Casey's image tormenting him.

At least that was the plan. But so far, this sudden burst of energy wasn't helping him forget her halo of bright hair or the stubborn lift to her chin. Waking at all hours of the night, he felt her warm lips on his, her soft breasts pressing into his chest.

What was he thinking? He owed it to Dorothy's memory to be loyal. He wasn't comfortable examining his feelings, but surely, what he felt toward Casey was nothing more than a certain likeability factor. Maybe they both just needed a release from their sex drives—nothing complicated about that.

Thinking of her latest note inside the pocket of his shirt didn't help either. He stopped chopping a moment to adjust the knotted kerchief he'd tied around his forehead for a sweatband. No need to take the paper out of his pocket, he remembered it word for word.

'*Stop and smell the roses, life is gone before you know.*
'*Treasure each precious moment, before you let it go.*

'Stop to smell the roses, push away the thorns.
'Every storm brings rainbows and after every night—the morn.
'Stop and smell the roses, remembering love grows cold
'And the loneliness inside you is what the future has to hold.'

What did she mean? Was she giving up on love? No. She was too spirited to do that. And she had a lot to offer any man. He recalled the love he had seen in her expression when she watched her son. He'd also felt her involuntary answer to his own needs, the banked passion beneath that cool exterior when she kissed him back. Until she pulled away.

Throwing down the ax, he stalked toward the corral. The big gelding sauntered forward to greet him, pushing his soft nose against the top of Matt's shoulder.

His life and the way he lived it satisfied Matt. How had Casey drawn him to her so fast and furiously? No woman, not even Dorothy, had ever made him feel turned inside out like this. Like his guts had been yanked out, leaving a shell behind.

A groan of anguish escaped as he put his head down on the rail of the corral. Loving someone left you open to pain and emptiness.

He'd never known losing someone could hurt so long and so fiercely and there was no way he would ever chance that again. He had nothing left to give anyone, anyway. He kicked a stone with his booted toe. God, what had he been thinking when he kissed her?

Casey was an adult, same as he. But she couldn't know what pain really was since she hadn't lost anyone yet. Divorce was not the same as killing someone you loved like he had killed Dorothy, his unborn son, and Manuel, who he'd grown up with and who had been like a brother to him.

The memories continued to fester like an open wound he'd been living with for eight long years. Dot hadn't wanted to be pregnant in the first place. She did it for him. If he hadn't decided to take that back road on the way to the hospital that night, the drunk would not have slammed into them. Oh God, why didn't he see him coming in time to swerve away? All his fault—everything.

He dragged his mind away from the tattered memory and made his thoughts center on Casey. He understood the sense of emptiness revealed by her poetry. She had to feel rejected by that jerk of a husband. He apparently had washed his hands of both of them.

Matt reached out and stroked the horse's nuzzle. "Your name's Smokey now. Got that?" He grinned as the horse spread his lips wide in answer.

Odd little boy, Jake. What the lad needed most was a dose of grit he could only get from being around a man. Casey was strong in her own way, but soft when it came to her son. Hell, how could she head the boy in the right direction when she didn't have her own bridle set firmly between her teeth?

Here he was, getting involved in someone else's problems. He would be smart to go back out on the line and keep his distance from Casey Nichols. Yet, knowing she was away from the ranch on a shopping trip to town left an emptiness inside him, and he couldn't wait for her return.

♞

Casey and Jake spent the day in Parker, shopping first, followed by the doctor's appointment. It was something she both looked forward to and dreaded. Would the doctor confirm that Jake was getting well? Observing Jake with as dispassionate a point of view as possible, Casey thought that he did appear improved since they left Phoenix. His skin showed the slightest hint of a tan, his cheeks were filling out, and the bruised looking skin under his eyes had disappeared.

The jitters descended upon her in the doctor's waiting room, but she tried to hide it from Jake by losing herself in a magazine. Once they were ushered inside the examining room, he stood straight without trying to become invisible, and he didn't stutter. Surely the doctor would have to admit he was making progress.

"Judging from the records you brought with you, Mrs. Nichols, your son's health has improved amazingly."

Casey breathed a huge sigh of relief as the doctor patted Jake's head with gentle hands.

She looked down to see if her feet stayed on the floor, since she felt like she could walk on a cloud, hearing vindication of her decision to move to Colorado.

"He loves it up on the mesa. The air is crisply cold at night, even in the summer, and the days are heaven."

The doctor smiled. "I know. Best place in the world you could have taken him. Of course, there is always the problem of isolation. In an emergency—for example, are you prepared for winter? They get pretty hard sometimes."

"We've got that all covered." Casey assured the doctor before he alarmed Jake who was listening intently. She had spoken with Jake many times about his illness and answered any questions he asked, but she didn't want him turning into a worrier or a hypochondriac.

When they left the doctor's office, they were both in high spirits.

They crossed the street to a little park. He sat at her side only for a moment before darting up, running around like a dragonfly, and touching every branch on the trees he could reach. He ran to sit on a swing, jumped and tried to smell a butterfly that touched down on a nearby bush, almost as if challenging her to stop him, since the doctor had pronounced him better. He skipped, arms in the air, through a flock of pigeons and laughed as they fluttered up in noisy annoyance and then settled calmly back on the sidewalk.

Casey let him go. He deserved to have a little fun after being ill for so long. He ran toward another little boy who knelt to sail a toy boat in the pond. Since she didn't shout a caution about not getting too close to the edge of the water, he looked back at her with surprised grin.

She grinned back. Mother Quail was trying really hard to let go.

The boys became friends immediately and rushed off to play together, while the child's mother walked toward Casey.

"What a sweet little boy," she said when she came within speaking distance.

"So's yours," Casey said.

The woman laughed. "No one has ever put the words sweet and David in the same sentence before. Thanks anyway. I'm Helen." She stuck out her hand.

Casey shook it and introduced herself, liking the tall willowy brunette at once.

"I've never seen you in the park before," Helen said. "Usually the only people who come here are those who go to Heart's Desire." She stopped, obviously dismayed at what she said.

"Are you referring to the wing for the terminally ill children? I hadn't realized they have one in this hospital. I worked as a volunteer at a clinic in Phoenix for several years before we moved away." She gestured toward Jake. "My son has asthma, but the doctor told us today he's doing fine. We're staying about sixty miles away so we drive to the clinic for his checkups. For the more elaborate tests we'll have to go to Center City, I'd imagine."

"Whew! I thought I'd put my foot in it that time. Mothers don't want to talk about their kids being in Heart's Desire and I don't blame them."

"Do you live around here?"

"Close. My husband died several years ago. I worked as a nurse before we met and gave it up to raise our son. But I went back to work after his death. Lucky for me, my sister lives nearby to sit with David. Today's my day off."

"Are there many terminal children in the unit?" The thought was not going to go away, at least until she had all the facts. She missed being with the kids. They were amazingly upbeat and made her feel needed during those dark years in her marriage. She brought videos and DVDs for the kids to watch. Every afternoon the nurses let her microwave popcorn for them and the remembrance of sitting at the side of each one in turn and talking to them about their families still brought a warm glow and tears to her eyes.

"Sometimes a few children, sometimes a dozen. Not more than that though. We don't have the facilities for many more."

Casey recalled how close Jake had come to needing such a place at the beginning of his life. She shuddered and pushed the wayward thoughts away.

Helen stood, extending her hand again. "Enjoyed the visit. When you come back for the next appointment drop in on the ward. I'll probably be working, at least most nights. Maybe you would like to volunteer at our Heart's Desire. We could sure use the help. Mothers bring that little extra touch that busy nurses don't seem to have time to offer the kids, no matter how much we try. We're stretched mighty thin."

"I'd like to, but we live too far away. We might have to move into town for the winter though."

Helen waved a hand. "Oh, I'm sure you could figure out something. Stay with David and me until you find an apartment. Our place is tiny, but I've got a rollaway bed and a couch."

"That might be a good idea. We'll see." The thought of leaving the ranch and Matt when winter came was a constant threat to her peace of mind. Yet, it had to happen eventually, unless she could persuade Matt that they would be safe in the cabin.

Helen collected her son and the two walked away. Jake ran toward Casey, excited and laughing. She lost herself in his rosy cheeks and shock of unruly blond hair that tumbled across his forehead. He shouted as he ran through another flock of pigeons.

"Come on, let's celebrate," she said.

She wanted to hug him in the worst way, but knew he didn't want that, not in public. He was growing up so fast after he had been her baby for so long.

Jake laughed at a nosy squirrel that ran in their direction only to veer off suddenly and dart up a tree, then he turned back to her. "I wanna pizza!"

Casey frowned. That wasn't on her list of nourishing foods. The doctors in Phoenix thought he might be allergic to strong spices, which could bring on an attack.

When she didn't answer, he spoke again. "I wish Matt was with us. He'd know the best place to go, I bet."

"Hey, kiddo, we don't call grownups by their first names, do we?"

He turned to her, his eyes so serious, with the hint of a grin lurking at the corners of his mouth. His nose had a smattering of freckles across it, like hers. Only she covered her freckles with makeup—or tried to.

"Remember? He told me to. Said Mister made him feel ancient." Jake rolled his tongue around the word, savoring it. "Does that mean I should call you Casey so you won't feel ancient?"

She laughed. "Not in this lifetime. Okay, you talked me into it. Let's do pizza."

How unwelcome, that fleeting twinge of annoyance. Or was it jealousy? Matt didn't know them, and he was intruding into their lives already. She tried to ignore the rush overpowering her senses as she remembered his firm, hard kiss, and the tenderness in his hands. Thoughts of him were constantly invading her peace.

"I need to find a computer store, pick up some more CDs for my laptop. Matt said I could recharge the batteries at his house, so that's taken care of. Then we are free for the day. Let's stay in town tonight. Catch a movie. How's that sound?"

"Great!" He grabbed her hand, ready to go.

CHAPTER 6

Heading toward the foothills the next morning, Casey's body screamed for rest. She ached in every place imaginable. Probably from holding herself so tight before they visited the doctor. Gradually she started relaxing and flexed her fingers on the steering, trying to convince herself she wasn't uptight any longer. They ate pizza the night before, without anything happening to Jake's breathing, and devoured buttered popcorn at the movies, something she had never allowed him to do before. It had been a long time since she relaxed and just had fun with him.

Reflecting on how seriously she had been taking life made her think of the book she was working on. If she could get back into her niche with her former publisher, she could avoid all contact with Jake's father. That would put her on top of the world. She felt some compunction over Jake not having a father figure, but she'd never had one and she survived. Besides, that had never been

Richard's role in his son's life anyway. She hoped that if he started a new family, he had learned something about children. And women.

Jake slept most of the way home. From time to time, she studied him. How would she protect him from life? Should she? He needed to go to school, to mix with kids his own age.

He woke up when they turned off the main highway onto the bumpy road heading to the ranch. When she drove down the little trail to their cabin and past Matt's house, there was a woman on his porch. She stopped sweeping long enough to wave a hand in greeting to them.

"Paco and Carmela must be back from their trip," Casey said.

"Can we go see them?"

"Probably. But let them get settled in first." Her voice dropped off when she saw the big, wine-colored Buick parked in front of her cabin. Her palms felt clammy and cold chills began at the back of her neck. The Nichols had found them. How? They might have written to tell her they were coming, but that way they never would have caught her off guard. Their visit couldn't mean anything positive. Would they try to reclaim their grandson again? They had to know Richard didn't want his son. What if Richard had changed his mind and wanted them back? Shivers of panic washed over her. Could he *make* her return? She didn't see how.

Since she didn't smell his aftershave, he probably hadn't come along. Casey raised her chin, threw her shoulders back and braced for a confrontation. In the past, she had always backed down, conceding to their combined authoritative personalities.

Jake scooted up straight to look out the car window. "It's the Colonel and Ma'am. Why are *they* here?"

She had never said anything negative to Jake about her in-laws. She didn't have to. He had always been very perceptive for his years. "Ah, Jake. They have asked you to call them grandfather and grandmother. Is that so hard to do?"

He turned to look at her. Blue eyes so like hers, arms folded across his chest. "Yep," he said with finality.

Casey laughed in spite of not wanting to. He had picked that up from Matt. No one else she knew spoke in monosyllables like in an old cowboy movie.

The long, sleek car was empty so they must have gone inside or were taking a walk.

She opened the screen door to let Jake in first. They sat at the kitchen table, when they might have made themselves at home on the couch and easy chair. It was hard knowing what to say to them and anything that popped out of her mouth sounded clumsy. "Hi. How in the world did you find us?"

"It wasn't easy. Don't you lock your door?" Mr. Nichols stood, offering his hand to Jake in greeting. "Hello, son. How's it going?"

Mrs. Nichols bent gracefully to bestow a dry kiss on Jake's cheek. "Hello, Jacob. Good to see you again."

Can't you give him a simple hug? Casey wanted to shout the question at them, but restrained herself. "We don't have to lock doors here." She hated the crankiness in her voice. She didn't ask about Richard. She hoped fervently they hadn't brought him and he wasn't outside walking around. "Hello, Sir...Ma'am," Jake stammered.

The couple appeared embarrassed at his stuttering, as if the boy had grown two heads. He barely stuttered any more since they had left Phoenix.

"Richy sends his love, dear. He couldn't make such a long trip on a short notice. But there are some serious issues he needs to talk to you about." Mrs. Nichols shot Casey an accusing look as if to say, it's your fault for moving so far away.

The news about Richard wanting to talk to her was not what she wanted to hear.

Richy. His parents were the only ones who would dare call him that. She would bet they never did it to his face. He wouldn't have been above giving them that cold, implacable stare that he had bestowed upon her more times than she wanted to think about. The nickname was a clear indication of how they had pampered him until he had lost all sense of responsibility for his own actions. They tried to fasten the nickname to Jake, but in the outset, she informed them that while she acceded to their wishes about her son's full name, she was going to call him by his middle name, Jacob or Jake.

"Can I make you a cup of coffee?" *Grit your teeth and be civil. At least try to set a good example.* At the Colonel's nod, she got up to put on the coffee. "How long have you waited?"

"Not long, actually. Were you out for a drive?" Richard's mother had a long, thin nose in keeping with the rest of her. She wore her purple-blue hair forced into tight waves that had probably gone out of fashion. Both his parents seemed to dwell in the past, which might have been the best years of their lives. The colonel was the only man she knew who still wore a World War II bristle-short haircut. Even Richard had called him Sir or Colonel.

"We went to Parker to check in at the clinic. There are hospital facilities in Center City too."

"That's how we found you. The clinic had sent a notice to remind you of Jake's appointment and the post office forwarded the letter to Richard. From there, it was only a matter of asking around about the ranch. We knew we would be too late to meet you in town so we asked directions and came out here. You did tell your neighbors about going to a ranch."

Drat! So she had. She didn't think they would remember.

"We looked in at the clinic. Not a bad little set-up," the Colonel said. "We also went to Center City to check out that hospital. We met Doctor Davidson there. We want only the best for Jacob." He looked at Jake who had slipped away to change into his shorts and tee shirt and now lay on the rug drawing in his notebook.

"That was good of you to check those places out, but unnecessary," Casey managed. "I wouldn't take Jake any place that was inferior. Besides, I doubt the hospital would share his records with anyone but me." She had never expressed herself so openly before, but she refused to hide in in anyone's shadow and wanted to say what she thought.

"We know, dear, we know." Mrs. Nichols said. "But my husband wanted to talk to the administration people and make sure everything was in order. One never knows in this Godforsaken wilderness."

"Harumph." The Colonel cleared his throat. "How is the coffee coming? Smells good." Making it clear he was impatient with woman-talk, he turned to Jake. "What's that you're doing, my boy?"

Jake held up his drawing for them to see. His eyes were hopeful, trusting. He had drawn trees in the background and what he remembered of a roadrunner in the middle of an open space.

Casey held her breath.

"Not bad, but a big lad like you, almost seven, you should be outside throwing hoops or tossing a baseball. Got a basketball or baseball handy? I'll toss a few with you. Your dad enjoyed that when he was your age."

Casey slammed a cupboard door shut. *Get a grip. No arguments in front of Jake.* She tightened her lips and spoke in as steady a tone as she could muster. "We couldn't bring all his toys. There wasn't room in the car. When he's ready, I'll get some outside things for him."

The colonel snorted under his mustache that bristled like his brush-cut hair. "So you can putter about with him, of course."

Like a female, he implied. Casey felt a warm flush rise from her neck to her cheeks. He never missed the chance to put her down. What did he mean, 'putter about'? She could throw a basketball or a baseball as good as most men and better than some. She had been a tomboy as a teen and played on the high school softball team as pitcher. She would be willing to bet Mrs. Nichols never touched a basketball in her life. In fact, the woman reminded her of one of the park pigeons complete with a long gray dress, a slightly puffed out chest, and a strut that showed contempt for lesser mortals.

"Jake, honey, take out the trash for me, will you?"

He leaped to his feet, no doubt relieved to go outside.

As soon as he slammed the door behind him and out of hearing range, Casey put her hands on her hips and glared at the two sitting so innocently at her table. "Haven't you noticed how much better he's looking? I won't have you staring down your noses at him."

"Jacob does appear quite well," Mrs. Nichols' voice was briskly conciliatory.

"Harumph. Still stutters, I see," was all the colonel could muster, plainly taken aback by Casey's strong stance.

"Today, seeing you, is the first time he's stuttered since leaving Phoenix," she snapped.

The Nichols both wore identical expressions of shock, eyes wide, mouths open. She had never spoken to them this way and felt a twinge of guilt, no doubt brought on by her early training in showing respect to elders. However, respect went both ways. Their constant belittling of her had grown bearable throughout the years, but no one was going to attack her son or the way she was raising him.

The door slammed again before the couple struggled out of their astonishment to answer. "I rode a horse. I s— sat on h—him all by myself." Jake's stammers skimmed along the surface of dead silence.

Casey wished he hadn't mentioned that. She'd been hoping he wouldn't say anything about Matt. Now she cringed, waiting for the fallout.

"Bully, lad!" his grandfather crowed then glared at his wife when she started to protest.

Now, after all this time, Casey knew who the man reminded her of. Teddy Roosevelt. Not as the president, but as one of the Rough Riders dashing off to Cuba to fight a war and carrying a big stick. She put her hand over her mouth to hide the threatening smile. Somehow, the idea comforted her, making him seem more human.

While they sipped the coffee and nibbled at her fresh cookies, they watched Jake play with his hand-held computer game.

"Dreadful thing for a boy to find interesting," Mrs. Nichols commented.

"Nearly as bad as drawing silly pictures—" The colonel began.

Before he could wind up with a long speech, Casey interrupted. "Whatever Jake is interested in, I'm all for it.

He's a bright kid, and he'll decide what's appropriate for
him." She remembered the times back in Arizona when he
dawdled all day in his pajamas, doing nothing but looking at
television.

"I've heard those games teach eye-hand coordination,"
the colonel conceded.

"That's true. Which in turns builds self-confidence and
keeps his mind working. Besides, he doesn't play at it often.
We take walks, go on picnics, and—" *Oh for heaven's sake,
here she was apologizing again for her son like she used to do.*

"It's time the boy went to a regular school. It seems to
me like you are molly-coddling him with home schooling."

"I've been told there is a regular school not too far
away, small but adequate, for the ranch kids. I checked into
that before I left Phoenix—"

"As to why we came all this way to find you," he
continued. The colonel's voice ran over her words,
knocking them down like building blocks. So typical. "We
found a new doctor in L.A. Tell her about him," he said to
his wife.

"He's an allergist, a specialist who comes from Europe.
Germany, I believe. Of course, we will pay for everything.
You may stay with us, if you like." *If you must*, the voice
implied. "It's a short flight from Phoenix to L.A."

The couple waited expectantly, while Casey glanced in
Jake's direction. Neither the Nichols nor Richard had
wanted to admit Jake had asthma. They regarded that as an
incontrovertible weakness, but allergies were explainable
and acceptable. Even adults suffered with them.

Jake pretended to concentrate on his game, but Casey knew he was listening. His face looked paler than usual and his hands trembled slightly. He was afraid she would send him away. *Oh Jake, honey, when will you learn that I will never abandon you?*

"No!" Had she shouted that out loud? The word exploded into the silence, which seemed to wrap around it, expanding the vibrant sound until it reverberated through the room like a note on a tuning fork. She caught Jake's grin before he turned back to his game.

"No?" Both voices chimed in together. The Nichols stared at her.

Moving in jerky steps toward the picture window, Casey gazed out across the yard in front of the cabin, taking solace in the soft greens of the foliage. Jake got up from his prone position in front of the fireplace to stand at her side, as if he wanted to give her moral support. Casey took his hand and turned to face his grandparents. *Stay calm, stay calm. Don't let them think you have turned hysterical again.*

"Look at him." She put her hand on Jake's shoulder. "He's improved a hundred percent since we arrived. The doctors at the clinic think a lot of his problem was stress. You both had to be aware that Richard and I weren't getting along. It's time we got it out into the open. You must have noticed the sign too." She squeezed her son's hand. "Jake might as well hear this too."

When the colonel made his harumphing noises, Casey didn't know whether to laugh or cry. How the whole family hated to show emotion. It was pathetic, an adult afraid to let someone in. She hoped to teach Jake that it was okay to be happy, mad, or sad and even to cry. It wasn't healthy to hide your feelings behind a mask.

"But..." The colonel sputtered. For the first time since she had known him, he appeared at a loss for words.

Casey saw new respect surfacing in their expressions. They had always walked over her before—when they weren't ignoring her completely. She had changed. They couldn't get away with treating her like that now. "I know you mean well, but I'm convinced I'm on the right track in bringing him to Colorado. He needs fresh, clean air, sunshine, good food, and no upsets." She kept her voice steady.

Their closed expressions told her nothing.

Mrs. Nichols spoke first. "We understand, dear. It's just that we are concerned and wish to help. Jacob may be the only grandson we'll ever have."

Were they implying that because she and Richard broke up he wouldn't have any more kids? She would bet he already had one in the basket with his girlfriend.

"Will you take the doctor's card? When you call, he has been kind enough to offer to discuss the case with you as a preliminary step."

Casey stared at them. This went beyond pushiness. That they were willing to discuss Jake's illness with a strange doctor surprised her. And the idea of not *if* you call, but *when* you call raised her hackles. No, Casey didn't like the sound of that at all.

How much trouble could they make for her and Jake? They had been sure enough of themselves to the point where they had already begun making arrangements in L.A. Had they set anything in motion in Center City? They wouldn't have bothered with Parker. The clinic was so small they must know it was only a stop-gap for Jake when he needed something in a hurry. They were both so rigid, so unbending. Had they always been that way? Imagination failed her when she tried to envision them as children. She began to understand Richard a little better and experienced a modicum of pity along with her stored-up anger.

"I know he's your grandson. I also know you have his best interest at heart, but the courts gave me full custody."

The colonel's mustache bristled, a sign he was holding himself in check. "We didn't contest that, even though we might have."

"Why would you, when Richard didn't?"

The couple looked embarrassed and stayed silent for a long moment.

"We'll leave the subject alone for now." Mrs. Nichols gave her a chilly smile that Casey felt sure would crack the woman's makeup.

They would be watching every step she made and second-guessing her all the way. Had they hired a private detective? She wouldn't have been surprised. "Thank you. We don't have much room, but you're welcome to stay the night." It was a token gesture and she prayed they wouldn't accept.

Mrs. Nichols' long narrow nose tilted in the air when she glanced around the room. "Oh no, we couldn't possibly."

"No, of course not," the colonel seconded, his voice sounding suspiciously placating.

They got up to leave, but they weren't through—not by a long shot. The words Mr. Nichols didn't speak rang out in Casey's head as if they had indeed sprung from his lips. She put her arm around Jake's shoulders while they stood outside on the porch, watching the pair climb into their car and back out of the driveway.

"You did great, Mom!" Jake raised his hand to high-five her. His wide smile brought a lump to her throat.

Had he been so sure she would cave on him? Make him go with the Nichols?

"I don't like them very much," Jake whispered, even though they were no longer in sight.

She drew a deep breath, wanting him to be honest about his feelings, but struggling with the need to teach him manners. "It's okay not to like someone, Son. That's your decision. But you must always show respect. They are older and your grandparents. I'm sure, in their own way, they love you."

"I guess so. But it's just us, right?" The worried little furrow between his eyes smoothed out, and he took a deep breath that ended with a spasm of coughing.

She sat him down and went inside to get his medicine and a glass of water. She poured out a pill in his palm. "There, is that better?" She handed him a paper towel to wipe the perspiration from his forehead. "I love you, Jake. I will always be with you, to take care of you. Remember when I said I'd help carry your books when you went to college?"

Her smile echoed his at their shared joke. Had she done right by Jake? Or was the greatest doctor money could buy the best thing for him?

♞

Later that night, Casey sensed something wrong and woke with terror thudding in her chest. Jake! Had he called out to her? It was then she heard his labored breathing. She leaped out of bed, her feet tangling in the covers. Holding on to the bedside, she kicked them away. Jake sat crumpled in a heap against her open bedroom door.

"Oh God! Jake! Jacob! Wake up. Please wake up." She took hold of his shoulder and shook gently, listening to the whistling in his lungs. A very bad sign. She could heat water to use in the vaporizer but that might not help at this stage. And it would waste precious time. His face was pale and the veins in his closed eyelids looked like tiny blue spider webs.

Her heart raced in her chest, making it hard for her to breathe as well. Taking a deep breath to calm herself, she fought to find the control she needed. In the past, she had always taken him to the hospital, which had never been far away, and they gave him a shot and put him on oxygen.

The Parker clinic, that was where she needed to be. They would give him a shot to soothe his bronchial passages. She couldn't drive, though, and leave him unattended in the back seat.

Casey prayed while pulling on her jeans and buttoning her blouse. Matt would help. She looked toward his house, hidden by trees and too far away to see if a light burned. He could drive while she held Jake. She scooped up her son and ran out of the house, fighting the panic that threatened to overwhelm her. She had always had someone nearby to call on for help. She sat him in the car, closed the door and spun her wheels taking off up the trail to the house.

Matt would help. He had to. He was the type of man you could lean on when you needed him, and she never needed anyone more.

CHAPTER 7

It seemed to take forever to make it up to the circular drive in front of Matt's house. When Casey sighted the entrance around the last bend in the lane, she honked the horn and flashed the headlights off and on.

Matt, shirtless, Levis half-unbuttoned, vaulted over the porch railing almost before she braked the car. He jerked the door open.

Casey didn't need to say a word. By the looks of his troubled, steady gaze he had obviously sized up the situation in a second.

"*Que pasa?* What is happening?" Carmela asked as she and Paco appeared next to Matt.

Jake opened his eyes, startled by the sudden commotion. "Matt. Where's your horse?" He managed to whisper.

"Hey, pard. How's my buddy? Hang tough, we're going to the doctor." He reached over Jake to grasp Casey's shoulder, giving her a gentle shake. "You hang in there too." He turned to Paco and Carmela, waiting nearby. "Bring my wallet and grab a shirt for me." He sat on the steps to pull on the boots he brought outside with him. "Get a wrap for Casey and a pair of Paco's slip-ons, she's barefooted. *Andele*! Hurry!"

Paco and Carmela raced into the house. Matt's ringing authority, his taking charge of the situation without needing explanations, made Casey sigh with relief.

"I'll drive you to Parker," he said. "It'll be faster in my car. You need to hold him." Matt's strong hands helped her out of the car. When she tried to stand, she sagged against him. It was as if her trembling legs belonged to someone else. He shushed her protests, picking her up easily, while Paco opened the passenger side of the Jeep. Matt set her down, touching her cheek with the side of his hand.

"I won't let anything happen to him. We'll get there, I promise." He turned back to her car to fetch Jake. For a brief moment, Matt stood still, legs apart, looking down at the boy. Casey's heart almost stopped, until she heard her son's breathing.

She held out her arms. Not more than a heartbeat passed before he brought Jake around front to lay him half on, half off her lap. His hand lingered briefly on her shoulder, a tight grip that normally would have made her cringe, but she barely felt it.

"Hold on, Casey. You can do it. He's breathing shallow, but he's breathing." Matt's husky voice broke. He turned away when Carmela came running down the steps, throwing the things he had asked for in the back seat.

"Good, thanks. Call the clinic. You will find the number on the telephone book cover. I think Mom wrote it there for emergencies. Tell them the problem so they'll be ready for us." He spared a moment to slip Paco's shoes on Casey's bare feet.

"*Vaya con Dios, pobricito.*"

Casey wasn't sure if Carmela's whisper was aimed at Jake, her, or both of them. The last thing she saw in the side mirror was the couple standing in the driveway.

The bumpy graded-dirt road seemed to shake the whole car. Instead of harming Jake, it seemed to help him. He suddenly started breathing easier. She glanced over his head at Matt and their gazes locked for an instant.

They didn't speak. Matt was concentrating on the hilly road, while Casey cuddled Jake. As soon as Matt turned onto the four-lane highway, he floored the accelerator.

"I don't usually fall apart this way," she said. "It's just that a hospital has never been so far away and for a while there I panicked."

"That's understandable. But his color's better already." Matt reached over and covered her hand with his against Jake's back. The feel of his warm, callused palm soothed her.

They sped through the star-filled night, the slash of headlights penetrating the black void ahead of them. The only sound between them was Jake's breathing.

"Does this happen a lot?" Matt asked, finally breaking the silence.

Casey swallowed around the tightness in her throat and kissed the top of Jake's head. "Not so much. But Richard's parents tracked us down and came to visit today."

"And?" He prompted.

"They wanted Jake to go back with them for a professional consultation. They'd found an amazing new doctor—or so they said."

"Did Jake think you would let him go?"

"No, I don't think so, but it still made him nervous. No one stands up to the colonel, not even Richard. I never did before, either."

"It must have made Jake proud when you faced him down."

Casey smiled, remembering the sudden light in Jake's eyes, that mischievous grin as he heard her telling the Nichols that she was taking care of her son and thank you, but no, she didn't need their assistance.

"You said the colonel. Do you mean Jake's grandfather?"

She knew he was whispering, his voice low and husky, in an attempt to avoid disturbing Jake. "Yes, he's retired military. Everyone steps to his march. I suppose Jake might have worried that I'd cave in."

"But you said no."

"Darned right I did, in no uncertain terms. I told them Jake was getting better and that I could take care of him perfectly well. We didn't need any more fancy doctors poking and prodding him." She leaned her head away to hide the tears that trickled from under her eyelids.

He touched a hand to her cheek. "Hey, don't cry. You did good."

"I want to think I did the right thing, bringing him here, but maybe—"

"That's bull and you know it." His fingers lightly caressed her chin and turned her toward him. "You did the best thing by refusing their help, if you don't want it. I have seen an improvement in Jake, just in the time I've known you."

"Thanks. I think this episode was a delayed reaction to the Nichols' visit. One of the Phoenix doctors blamed much of Jake's problems on stress. He must have built up some fear while he listened to us talking."

"When he saw you weren't going to cave in to their demands, he collapsed. Inside where no one could see it."

"That's right. So at three in the morning he wakes up, unable to breathe."

"Think about it. You did the right thing, don't beat yourself up. It won't help Jake. He needs you to be strong, like you really are."

"Thanks for the pep talk." And she meant it. She leaned against the headrest and pulled Jake closer, tucking his head under her chin.

They traveled in silence the rest of the way. Several times, she caught Matt looking away from the ribbon of road in front of them to check on her. He must have broken every speed limit in the books getting to town. When they pulled up in front of the hospital emergency entrance he laid on the horn. Then in a flash, he was at her side, helping her out.

"Want me to take him?"

"I think you'd better. I'll need to fill out papers."

Jake woke long enough to wrap his arms around Matt's neck, causing Casey to swallow past a new lump in her throat. Matt's long-legged strides ate up the pavement as he rushed to the door. A crew of attendants, apparently forewarned by Carmela, hurried forward. They laid Jake on a gurney and Matt went back with Jake to the ER waiting area until a doctor could get there.

At the front desk, Casey hurriedly filled out the forms and showed her insurance cards. Without giving it a thought, she put down Matt's name as an alternate to hers instead of Richard's. By the time she finished with the paperwork and pushed back the curtain in Jake's room, the doctor had just arrived. She filled him in on what had happened. Jake looked so small under the white hospital sheets and the oxygen mask over his nose. As soon as they got him stabilized, they would probably put an oxygen tent over him. That always scared him.

Matt came up beside her, wrapped his arm around her shoulders, and rested his chin lightly on top of her head in a comforting gesture, much like she did with Jake. She felt a rush of gratitude for his support.

Suddenly she saw a streak of Milky Way stars speed across the ceiling then everything went black.

CHAPTER 8

Casey awoke lying on a strange bed in what was obviously a hospital room. She sat up, looking around and saw a small form in a bed on the other side, by the window. Matt sat nearby, eyes closed, head propped by a pillow behind him.

She tossed the cover from her legs and struggled to her feet. "Is that Jake?"

"Whoa, Casey," Matt said, instantly alert. "He's doing fine."

His warm smile dissolved the panic that had assaulted her upon awakening. "I can't believe it. I must have blacked out. I've never done that before. I'm so embarrassed." And glad the Nichols were not around to witness this.

"Hey, let up on the Super Mom idea, will you? You've had a rough go."

She wobbled on unsteady legs toward the other bed to see Jake.

Matt was on his feet in a second, standing by her side for support. "The doctors say he'll be okay. I'll call for someone to come and talk to you."

It was then she remembered putting Matt's name down as someone who the doctors could also talk to. How odd that she did that automatically.

Jake appeared so fragile, lying in the big white bed. When the doctor came in, all smiles, Casey knew Jake would be fine. The doctor was a youngish man, not much older than she was, with an air of importance wrapped around him as natural as the white jacket he wore.

"Mrs. Nichols." He reached forward to shake her hand. "Mr. Tyree has been filling me in. Seems your son had some stress tonight, bringing on his attack."

"Yes, he's been getting better since we moved to Colorado. He hasn't even needed to use his inhalers lately."

"I suppose the doctors in Phoenix explained about the two types of asthma, *extrinsic* and *intrinsic*. Children usually develop the extrinsic variety, which has a good outlook as far as not expanding into serious respiratory and cardiac conditions. Your son looks delicate, but he is tougher than you imagine. He has an excellent chance of eventually outgrowing asthma. Many children do."

In spite of his slow, pedantic way of speaking, almost as if she were mentally deficient, Casey inhaled his words like ambrosia. She wanted to hug him. "No one's bothered to explain much to me, although I have asked. I've looked up a lot in medical books and on the Internet but it isn't the same as someone like you telling me."

"Good. Some doctors do not approve of sharing too much information. Often parents put their own slant on what we tell them. Remember the old adage, a little knowledge can be dangerous? I disagree. Knowledge empowers patients and their families, enabling them to come to a better understanding about a disease or condition."

"In the past, he's had a tent with oxygen and a tube down his throat. He didn't need that?"

The doctor shook his head. "Not at all. His vital signs were normal by the time you brought him in. He was breathing lightly and had no fever."

"When can I take him home?"

He checked the chart and looked at his watch. "I'd say early afternoon. Let him sleep for now. It is the best recuperative power there is. I'll leave instructions at the nurse's station." He put his hand lightly on her shoulder and then, with a glance at Matt standing so protectively close, he backed off slightly.

"Thank you doctor, you've been a big help in relieving my mind."

"You're doing fine with your son. Keep him away from stress, that's the main thing. Those bronchial passages will close right up on him. In my opinion it is something he will outgrow as he learns to handle the stress. It's your job to teach him that."

Casey held out her hand. "Thanks again for all you've done."

"Why don't you two have a cup of coffee in the cafeteria," the doctor suggested. "We examined you and it seems your blood pressure went a little high, which probably caused you to faint. Temporary stress, nothing serious. You'll be fine."

"I hate to leave Jake. What if he wakes up and wants me here? He'll be scared."

"We've given him a mild sedative. He'll sleep peacefully for hours."

When the doctor bustled away, Matt led her to a chair, his hand on her arm.

"Thanks. I'm okay, honest. I don't know what happened. I've never fainted in my life."

"How about that coffee? I could sure use a cup,"

"Well...I guess."

"You heard the doc. Let's go for the coffee and then you can come back here and get a few hours' sleep. You look like you could use it."

"You sure know how to charm a girl, cowboy. Are you saying I look a bit frazzled?"

"I didn't—" He stopped in mid-sentence and then must have seen she was teasing.

He was not used to humor, she could tell. At least not her style of it. She bent and kissed Jake on the forehead, covertly feeling for any hint of fever. His skin felt cool, his breathing was normal, and his color good.

Matt led her to a glassed-in terrace of the cafeteria and, when she was seated, went back to place their order. She watched him walk across the floor of the cafeteria as if he owned the world. Slips of forgotten memory came to her now that Jake was out of trouble.

Matt with his Levi's half-buttoned, an arrow of fine, dark hair starting below his navel and reaching downward. She had wondered before what the color of his skin was without the tan. Now she knew. His shirt off, his chest hard and brown, he jumped over the railing, carrying his boots. Casey blushed at her wayward thoughts and wondered how she had time in that stressful situation, to notice all this and catalog it for later. She was glad he wasn't near to see her. He seemed intuitive at times, almost as if he could read her thoughts, which proved very disconcerting, since he seemed so pragmatic and not particularly in tune to the feelings of others.

By the time he returned to the little metal table, Casey had regained control of her thoughts. He had bought pieces of warm apple pie and coffee.

She toyed with her pie, teasing it with the fork. "Thank you, Matt. Thanks a lot for being with us tonight."

He nodded, sipping his coffee, plainly not knowing how to respond to gratitude.

She decided to change the subject since he seemed so uncomfortable. "Did I ever tell you about Heart's Desire?"

He shook his head.

"Oh, well, coming here to this hospital reminded me of it. It's usually in a separate wing of a hospital where the terminally ill children reside. Volunteers help the children cope when their own families get crazy about their illness."

"Why is it called Heart's Desire? That seems pretty contradictory."

"It really isn't. The volunteers try to give the kids what they most want. Kind of like granting a special wish. There are agencies to help fund this too." Although, it was hard to explain why it was so important, she wanted him to understand. Then a thought bubbled up from where it had been hiding. "I had a crazy idea in there while we talked to the doctor. About the Heart's Desire wing in Center City and maybe here, too."

Matt waited for her to finish, a politeness she wasn't used to yet.

She took a deep breath. "I bet the last request from some of these kids would be to live on a ranch a week or so, talk to animals, touch horses, maybe even ride them if possible."

He cleared his throat. "I see where you're going with this. It's an interesting idea, but impractical. The ranch is sixty miles from here and isolated. Then there are the insurance costs."

Casey found words rushing into her mind to help overcome his resistance. Her relief in Jake's close call made her eager to give something back to others. She reached across the table to touch his hand. "I volunteered to work with the unit in Phoenix. They were such great kids. You would never know they were terminal, and that everyone had given up on them. They helped me keep my act together much more than I could have possibly helped them." At his doubtful expression, she hurried on. He hadn't said no. "I'll bet your mom and dad would love to get involved with the kids. Don't forget Paco and Carmela. There wouldn't be many at a time, and they'd have a nurse in attendance."

"It sounds like you've given the idea a lot of thought."

"I haven't, really, not until this very moment. When the doctor said Jake could outgrow his problem, it made me think of the kids who will never outgrow theirs. You said you had buildings on the place that you never used anymore. We could fix up the bunkhouses."

"We?"

"Well, heck, you'd need help. Carmela can't do it all. I bet she'd love it though."

"Oh not a doubt, she'd be crazy for the idea. As it is, she doesn't have enough to keep her busy, but..."

Casey could tell by the frown on his face that he was thinking hard about it. Should she push or let it alone for now? She never was too good at keeping her patience.

"How many do you suppose they'd let come out at one time?" he asked. "It just sounds dangerous to me. What shape are the kids in? I mean, they wouldn't bring them out in stretchers would they? I don't see how a ranch would be of much help in that case."

Good, he was willing to talk about it and listen. "Probably they would start with two or three at the most. The hospital administrators have to check it out first and they are very cautious. I've seen children who you'd never know anything was wrong with them except for their bald heads and pale skin."

"I did mention insurance, didn't I?"

"Yes, you did. Which is a sensible concern. However, the Heart's Desire Association has separate attorneys and funds to take care of accidents or injuries. Otherwise, the hospital wouldn't let the kids even visit home anymore. That would be a tragedy. On the other hand, some live too far away to go home and their parents have to come visit them in the hospital. Some don't have money for that."

"It's a hard concept to grasp right now. Let's table the idea, okay?"

"All I ask is that you think it over." It was time to change the subject again. "You must know every inch of this town. You've lived near here all your life."

"Not much to know. Not many things have changed. Like the pie?" he added. He finished his piece and seemed to be eyeing hers. She pushed the plate toward him, and he grinned, a slow smile that made her heart race.

"I used to think any pie was good, until I tasted yours."

"I remember, you said Dorothy and your mother didn't bake but preferred to work outdoors." As soon as she said the words, she wanted to recall them, seeing it was a mistake.

His expression turned remote, closed, his eyes inscrutable beneath dark brows.

Seconds ticked by, until Casey thought Matt wouldn't respond.

"I don't want to talk about that."

Casey flushed. "I apologize if I said anything offensive. It's just that I don't know anything about your life. You know about mine."

He was silent a long moment. "That was your choice, not mine. I never asked, or tried to pry."

Is that what he thought her conversation was? Prying? The chip started to grow on her shoulder, and the weight of it pressed downwards. She wasn't ready to open her heart to anyone, but if she did, it would never be just because someone had shown her and Jake a little kindness. Trusting before, thinking she knew a man inside and out, and not knowing him at all, had left her doubting her judgment. At least it was plain this man wasn't her kind of hero at all.

They finished their coffee in silence, with the growing companionship between them disappearing.

"Want to see the folks' house?" he asked as if extending a peace offering.

"I'll have to take a peek in at Jake first. He may be awake. We wouldn't be long?"

He shook his head and she had to resist the urge to brush back the lock of dark, wavy hair that fell across his forehead.

They checked on Jake. He was lying in the same position, snoring slightly as he did when he was comfortably asleep. Casey brushed her fingers over his cheek then kissed his temple.

"We'll be back within the hour," Matt told the nurse.

Daylight peeked softly through the blinds on the windows as he steered Casey out of the room. Once in the

Jeep, he drove through the tree-line streets with a sure familiarity. "There she is." They stopped in front of the house. It was obviously empty, with that forlorn, lost appearance of closed houses, when no one has been inside for a long time. "They bought this house way back before we got electricity out on the ranch and before we had the cattle. We used to spend some winter months here."

"When did you say they'd be back?" She tried to keep her questions politely distant so he wouldn't as accuse her of prying again.

"This fall—they won't stay away past October. They love the winters here. Pop taught me to cross-country ski. Once I discovered there was a way to go places besides on horseback, life on the ranch wasn't so bad. Not much to do in the middle of winter out there."

"Is there an ice skating rink in town?" She thought that if they had to move off the ranch this winter, they could come here and she could teach Jake how to skate. "Jake would love it, he's never seen snow, so ice skating would be like magic to him."

"Everyone here uses the lake when it freezes over. We have a small pond behind the ranch house. It freezes solid. Too shallow to be dangerous."

Had he forgotten that he didn't want them to stay during the winter? She sneaked a look at him, but couldn't read the expression in his eyes.

They rode around town a few more minutes, and he pointed out landmarks until he must have seen she was growing restive, wondering about Jake.

Back at the hospital, they stood beside Jake's bed just as he began a gigantic stretch and opened his eyes. His face lit up when he saw them. Casey was surprised not to feel a slight hint of jealousy when her son looked so adoringly at Matt.

"You want to get him ready?" Matt asked. "I'll bring the Jeep around front and wait out there for you."

Jake would hardly hold still for her while she helped him with his clothes, so any notion she had that she could keep him quiet was out of the question. When they pushed out of the swinging doors and walked outside, Matt stood waiting with the car door open.

She felt a tremor from the top of her head to her toes as she stared at him—his wide shoulders, narrow hips, slightly bowed legs. She couldn't stop the grin when she noticed women staring at him as they passed. She didn't blame them.

He swept his black Stetson off in a gesture of welcome. "Hi, pard. What took you so long? I was ready to go in there and lasso some ornery nurse who might be holding you back."

She and Jake laughed. Matt obviously enjoyed engaging in "cowboy talk" with Jake and the boy loved it. Jake started talking a mile a minute, saving her from having to carry on a conversation. She couldn't have spoken then if she had wanted to. Her throat had constricted at the way Jake looked at them both—as if they were a *family*.

On the ride home, he had a hundred questions to ask about what happened. He had blanked out on everything after they left the cabin.

Matt teased and talked to him, but remained distant from her, retreating behind those deep brown eyes.

Casey understood. She had come too close to his center, that hidden place he kept sacrosanct, enduring the pain that was there already but afraid to allow any chance of new hurt to come in. Would he ever let anyone inside again?

CHAPTER 9

After they returned from their night in the hospital, Jake prattled on about Matt for days, and wondered why he didn't visit. Finally, Casey grew impatient.

"Just forget it, Jake. If you must know, we don't see eye to eye on a lot of things."

"How come? I thought you was friends."

She didn't bother to correct his grammar. Sometimes she thought he knew better but it was his way of teasing her to see if she paid attention. "We were learning to be friends. Sometimes friends disagree. That doesn't mean he has forgotten *you*. He'll ride over one day, just give him time. He's very busy with his cowboy stuff."

She missed Matt too, more than she wanted to admit.

The next morning she heard a knock on the door. A brisk, peremptory knock, loud for so early. She opened the door to Matt, standing on the porch, hat in hand.

"I know it's early, but..."

Casey saw herself from his point of view and tried to smooth her uncombed hair. She had barely finished brushing her teeth. She snapped her bathrobe wrong and she was barefoot. Worst of all, totally without a trace of makeup. Why should she care? It wasn't as if she needed to impress him. He had to be impervious to anyone's charm.

"You look barely older than Jake." He hit his hat against his thigh, as if embarrassed at the personal observation.

"Thanks. I guess. What are you doing out so early? Did your cows stray into our yard?"

"Cattle. We call 'em cattle," he corrected, with a grin lurking at the corners of his mouth. "It's not what I'd call early. It's nearly eight. Been up since day break."

She laughed. "Don't pull that cowboy stuff on me, save it for Jake."

He laughed with her and dipped his head a bit to enter the doorway of the cabin when she beckoned him inside. He looked around and she guessed he wondered where Jake was.

"My son's a sleepy head. I don't understand where he gets it. I like to wake early, otherwise I've wasted half a day. But I did get up later this morning," she admitted, brushing back a stray lock of hair. "I worked on my book last night without realizing how late it had gotten."

"I love the morning. The cattle are frisky, the birds make all kinds of crazy sounds and the morning just smells good."

That was a lot from such a conversationally challenged cowboy. His mouth fascinated her with the sensuous way his lips turned up, his teeth a slash of white against the tan of his skin. His eyes crinkled at the corners in a very endearing manner. She tried to turn away from his mouth, to forget that kiss. His wry smile told her he remembered too.

The unabashed approval in his expression was something she found hard to accept. She clutched the robe tighter where she skipped the snaps in her haste to answer the door.

"You said you were too busy to visit us." She disliked the hostility in her voice, but she didn't care for his take-over attitude after he had closed the door in her face. Prying questions, indeed. She especially didn't want to involve Jake in some on-again-off-again friendship.

"I wanted to see Jake, ask him if he wants to go on another picnic, this time up at the house."

She had the feeling that, try as he might to personify Mr. Cool, her answer really mattered.

"Sit, please." She motioned toward the big chair. "Excuse the mess. We had popcorn last night while we played Scrabble and were so sleepy we didn't bother clearing away the dishes."

"Jake plays Scrabble? I thought that was for adults. The folks played it when they were here."

"It's a youth version, but I think he could play the regular one. He's learned from me that words have a special magic."

Matt walked over to touch the mantle with the silk flowers mixed with desert dry grasses. "The cabin looks fine to me. Good to see it lived in. Carmela keeps the ranch house so neat. I can't set down an empty glass but what she grabs it up and carries it away to wash."

"Maybe she doesn't have enough to keep her busy."

"You're probably right. I have her trained with my coffee cup, though. It could grow an inch of green stuff on top and she wouldn't touch it. I rinse it out and drink from the same cup all day. It's comfortable."

"You sound like a creature of habit."

He frowned. "Anything wrong with that?"

"I guess not. It's not me, though. I think habits get boring after a while."

"That's an immature attitude. Everyone needs a settled, peaceful existence."

Casey shook her head vehemently. "You're very sure of what everyone needs, aren't you? No one is going to catch me in that kind of comfort-trap again. Richard had our lives all planned from our linen and dishes to our vacations ten years into the future."

"That does sound a little restrictive," he admitted.

"That's not the half of it. When Jake came along—weak and sickly as he was in the beginning—Richard's serene life fell apart, like unrolling a ball of yarn. It became untidy, with stray ends sticking out that he couldn't tuck away. It threw him for a loop and he never recovered."

Matt sat with his back ramrod straight, even in the easy chair. He reminded her of an old John Wayne movie. He was predictably the same, deeply conservative, right guard, old school hero-type. That should be an interesting facet of his personality to grapple with, since they couldn't manage to agree on whether habits were beneficial or not. She never had a semi-flirty contentious discussion with a man before. Richard would not have tolerated it for a second. It was proving quite interesting. She enjoyed the repartee with Matt.

His voice interrupted her thoughts. "There are good habits and bad ones, I'd say. Taking care to have food on the table for your family, feeding stock when they depend on you, paying your bills on time and—"

"All right, all right," she said, holding her palms toward him in a gesture of surrender. "I get the picture." She laughed. "Salt of the earth, middle America, apple pie and iced tea. Do you have framed pictures of presidents on your walls?"

His eyes narrowed and he regarded her with what she perceived as pretended indignation. Behind his look, she saw a pensive awareness. Did he really think about her words? Did he want to know what made her tick? He probably wouldn't like what he uncovered.

When her mother died from cancer, and her father couldn't take it and left her with an aunt, she had decided there was no such thing as a safe haven. Then she met Richard and thought he had to be the security she craved, which proved to be false. Now she was no longer looking for a sense of security, seeing it as an empty promise no one ever kept. That concept seemed to be working for her. Otherwise, she would never have had the courage to leave Richard.

"I'm convinced nothing like safety and security exists," she said. "Like most women, I want a little romance with the apple pie and cozy fire at night. I want to feel special, to feel that someone can't live without me. I want someone who isn't afraid to show me that, tell me."

"Hmm. Every woman I know seemed content with a man to take care of her, put food on the table, and—"

"How many women have you known, if I may be so bold to ask? Your mother? Your wife? The other ranch wives around here, if there are any around? I'm glad for them that they didn't expect much from life." That sounded cruel. How would she know what gave the women joy? How could she explain? Her words came out as superficial, but the meaning was so hard to justify to someone who didn't want to understand. She wanted passion and fire and she wanted gentleness and caring. Maybe that was too much to ask from a man.

He looked as if he would like to be anywhere but where he was.

"Anyway, Richard wasn't what I needed."

"He hasn't come to see you yet. Do you think his parents told him where you are?"

"I suppose so. But it wouldn't matter. I imagine he's beginning a new life for himself." She prayed this was so, or Richard would track them down to claim part of Jake's life eventually. It wasn't anything she wanted to think about just now.

"You said having a son like Jake threw him off stride. What does that mean? Wasn't he glad to have a child—a son?"

She wanted to tell him it was none of his business, the way he'd cut her off when she got a little too close. Still, his question didn't feel offensive, and he hardly seemed the kind to ask frivolous questions just to be talking. Maybe this was important to him to understand because of his affection for Jake. It was obvious her son had captured an admirer. Or was she giving it too much importance? It might be only curiosity on his part.

After she excused herself to bring them coffee, she settled onto the couch, tucking her legs up under her, and held the ceramic mug cupped between her hands.

The realization struck her that it no longer hurt to think about the past, hard as that was to believe. Richard had killed her love so thoroughly, she was no longer able to hate him.

She took a breath and let it out slowly. "Jake was a premature baby. I have never told anyone this, but before he was born, Richard and I had a terrible row. He had this routine for every day he after came home from playing executive at his father's brokerage house.

"Monday was racquet ball, Tuesday we played bridge with several couples at the country club. My duty on Wednesday was to entertain the women of our bridge-set in our home, Thursday we—well, anyway, so it went. Saturday nights we danced at the club. Every Saturday night. Richard was a clone of every man we knew. Young, old, middle aged, fat, skinny, it made no difference. They were all cut from the same piece of cloth."

She sighed. "I reached the point where I just couldn't take it. I didn't have one original thought in my head any longer. One Saturday I blew up. He was leaving on an out of state golf tournament that Sunday and I didn't think he should go. I was afraid the baby would come early while he was away."

Matt looked down at his boots and then up at her, his eyes brimming with sympathy.

By then, she would have liked to stop and put it all away again but she had gone too far. "We had a big fight. I refused to go to the club dance." When he opened his mouth, she shook her head. "There's more. I suspected he was seeing someone else, and that was one reason he liked the club so much. *She* was there. I accused him of being unfaithful and...he dragged me back to the bedroom and..." She struggled to keep the horror from coming back, what Richard had done to her in his rage.

"God, you've had it rough," Matt interrupted, as if he didn't want her to finish..

She forced herself to pull back from the memory of that night and made her voice sound normal. "I accept a share in the blame. He was the same person who courted me. I should have seen it. But I mistook his rigidity for stability, his control for support. That'll never happen again."

"The night Jake was born?" Matthew prompted.

"I threatened to bail out of the marriage. It was an accumulation of everything hitting me at once. He was the one who had wanted a child so badly—a son to carry on the family name. He blew up again, and when he raised his hand to hit me, I ran into the bathroom and locked the door. I heard him leave. He took the keys to both his car and mine, and his golf clubs, then left."

"With you so pregnant and upset?"

"Jake wasn't due yet. When the labor started early, I called 911 and when they didn't come as fast as I thought they should, I ran to the nearest house, a quarter mile away though it seemed a lot longer in the rain. The ambulance finally came and Jake was born a few hours later."

Matt reached his hand out and put it on top of hers in a comforting way. Casey held her breath, fearing the contact and yet craving it. When she finally pulled gently away, he leaned back, his eyes blazing.

"I'd like to get my hands on him right now," Matt said, his voice husky.

She thought those were the sweetest words she'd heard in a long time. "Thank you. We did get back together again and he was smooth as silk for a while."

"I would have thought having a son settled things for him. That he would be more...more decent toward you."

"No, not really. The first time Richard saw Jake through the nursery window, he looked like someone who had made a bad bargain and wanted his life refunded. We stayed together five more years, with me trying to hold the marriage intact. I wasn't taught to take the easy way out. But year by year it grew harder to work it out between us. He had a permanent mistress by then and his temper, never predictable, got more out of control. I actually became afraid to go to sleep sometimes when he was home."

"Didn't his folks know any of this?"

She shook her head. "No, I never spoke to them about it. They wouldn't have believed it of their darling boy anyway."

"Does he help financially?"

"He was very generous in his haste to be rid of us. In retrospect, that's all Richard had ever given of himself, monetary support. But I never know how long that will last and *I* need to take care of us. I don't want to accept anything from Richard ever again if I can help it and I sure didn't want him to know where we are. I really came up here to hide from everyone until I could get my act together."

"The financial help is something in his favor, I reckon."

"I worked for a while in a publishing house, illustrating poetry books. I discovered I would rather write than draw or paint. I sold a couple of children's books before I met Richard. One was selected for the Newberry Award," Casey said proudly.

Matt took a drink of coffee and ate a bite of the coffee cake she put in front of him. She enjoyed watching him eat.

A small crumb remained on the curve of his top lip. Casey licked her lips in an unconscious gesture. When his tongue touched upward to claim the crumb, she stared, mesmerized. Was she going crazy? She had the greatest urge to touch that crumb of cake, a feeling which made her squirm, imagining what he would think if he knew her thoughts. He exuded power and strength, but this no longer put her off as much as it should have. "You sure ask a lot of questions for a taciturn cowboy." She smiled and felt the chip on her shoulder melt like early snow.

It felt good to talk to someone, a disinterested bystander of sorts. "I'm going to earn my living, mine and Jake's. I don't need any ties to the past." *Not like some people,* she almost added.

"Seems to me your son needs a father."

"I hate to come off as bitchy, but we do just fine. He can live without a father. Single parents raise children successfully all the time. When we get over this rough spell of transition and Jake gets better, Richard might expect a share in his life at some time, but it will be too late then. Jake doesn't need leftovers any more than I do."

Matt slapped his hat against his knee again, as if wondering where to go with this. It was obvious he was uneasy speaking on such a personal level, but something must have made him ask the questions.

He stood, leaving her face to face with his long, denim-clad legs, staring at his belt buckle. She rose hastily.

He put a hand on her shoulder. His touch was strong, yet easy, as if he expected her to shrug it off. She stayed still, trembling beneath his fingers.

"You're a thoroughbred. You've been through all kinds of hell and still that little pointed chin sticks a mile in the air." Slowly, seductively, his gaze moved from her eyes down her throat and downward to the partially opened V of her robe. The smoldering flame she saw in his eyes both thrilled and terrified her, igniting a matching fire in the center of her core. The warmth quickly spread through her entire body.

He curled his hand behind her neck and pulled her close to him for a brief second before tilting her chin. As his mouth crushed hers, a groan escaped him, and he forced her lips open with his thrusting tongue.

Casey returned the kiss with reckless abandon, raking her hand over his broad back, feeling the muscles tense beneath her fingertips. He pushed his thigh between her legs and the rough denim of his pant legs sent sparks of searing heat racing up her spine. She pressed closer, hungry for more of the all-consuming warmth spreading through her body.

She twisted her fingers into the thick hair at the nape of his neck, his skin warm and leathery beneath her probing fingertips.

Matt broke the kiss, leaving her mouth bruised and burning. Holding her away from him, he looked deep into her eyes, and then released her abruptly and turned toward the door.

"Casey, I'd better leave. If you need anything..."

She licked her lips, resisting the urge to raise her fingers and touch them, at least until he was gone.

The truth slammed into her in a blow that was as dizzying as his kisses had been. He couldn't know, and she refused tell him, that she wanted him in a way she thought had been impossible. This strong, virile cowboy had a soft spot for her son as smooth and velvety as thistledown, and she appreciated his non-judgmental acceptance of Jake. In spite of his misgivings and the baggage he carried, he made her feel treasured. It was more than a physical attraction for her, but what was it for him? Just sex?

She wanted to know what exactly had happened in his past to make him so gun shy. Was it guilt of some kind? Maybe Carmela would be willing to shed some light on the details.

"Want me to get Jake? He'll be disappointed not to see you," she asked with a start. This was the first time she had ever forgotten about her son for even a moment. What if he entered the room while they were kissing?

"No, don't wake him just to say goodbye. I'll be back, if it's okay with you. Meantime, give some thought to the picnic. It would be good for Carmela and Paco too. They want to get to know you and Jake better."

"I'll let you know."

When he left, she suddenly felt a chill in the air—as if he had stolen the warmth from the day with his abrupt withdrawal.

CHAPTER 10

When Jake woke, Casey told him about the invitation to the picnic.

He jumped up and down and danced around as if he never went anywhere. It upset Casey for a few minutes, to think she might not be enough for her son.

True to his word, Matt returned several days later. By then, Jake was so hyped with the idea of visiting the main house that Casey didn't grab him in time to keep him from leaping off the porch to stand next to Matt who waited at the bottom of the steps.

Seeing Jake's bright eyes and laughing expression soothed away the last remaining jealousy, which she thought she had already conquered. "I'm not sure this is a terrific idea. He's getting hyper."

Matt and Jake gazed up at her from the bottom of the steps. He had brought Jake a hat like his, only a size too large. It pushed Jake's ears down so they looked pointed under the hat and the brim loomed across his forehead. "It was my hat when I was a kid," Matt admitted. "My mother never throws anything away."

Casey wanted to laugh—and cry—as they both stood there looking up at her with the same confusion on their faces.

Matt took Jake's hat off and ruffled his hair lightly in a gesture that went straight to Casey's heart, melting her defenses.

"Well, maybe it would be nice to get to know Carmela."

He must have understood her uncertainty—and the jealousy she tried so hard to fight. He stepped backward from Jake a pace and looked at her, his eyes unflinching in their appraisal. A muscle worked in his jaw. "I'm only offering friendship. Is that so bad?"

Did he consider kissing part of the friendship? It seemed to her as if he was setting the stage for a brief sexual fling with the idea that they would leave before winter set in. He was in for a surprise. She couldn't take the two sets of eyes staring at her so intently and turned back inside, slamming the screen door behind her.

Sitting at the kitchen table, Casey leaned her head down on her arms and let the tears fall—tears that had been a long time in coming. She held in the sobs, held tight so that Jake wouldn't hear her. In a minute she would be okay.

Something touched her shoulder, the hands too solid and firm to be Jake. She took a deep breath and raised her head. "You! You're invading my privacy."

"I know. It has to be rough, being mother and father. To tell the truth, at first I was scared of liking Jake. It's too late for that now. I do like him, and you, too. In fact I asked him to stay outdoors a minute and let us talk and by damn he did."

Matt grabbed a chair, straddled it, and leaned forward. He seemed so strong and solid, she wondered if the chair legs would hold him. She hoped Jake didn't see that. He would surely have to try it. "I'm grateful for your liking Jake, but I don't want him hurt."

"Him or you?"

"What do you mean?"

"Seems to me you're worried about your own feelings, and that's natural. Jake's tougher than you give him credit for. How can I hurt him?"

"By being there for him and then not being there," she blurted out, her eyes still brimming with tears, which she futilely tried to wipe away with her arm.

"I don't understand."

"You don't have room for friendships in your life. You're surviving on memories, protecting a dream, living on your remembrance of what was and can never be again."

"Good Lord! What a crazy idea! There's nothing wrong with being loyal, if you're referring to my memories of Dorothy. You're right though. I don't have space for anyone in my life. But I figure a friend doesn't take up that much room."

Pain simmered deep in his eyes, but he cleared his throat and took a couple of slow breaths, regaining his casual attitude. "Are you planning to live in Colorado the rest of your life?"

She sniffed. "I doubt it."

"Then I don't see a problem. It's kind of like those tumbleweeds out there, rushing around the desert, bumping into things, seldom catching hold. When you find a friend, you hold on for a while and then let go when the time comes. It's that simple and that's what I'm offering."

"Hells bells!" She exploded out of the composure she struggled so hard to maintain. "I wasn't suggesting anything else—I mean, I wasn't asking you to..." *Marry me?* "I mean, just because we kissed is no reason..."

She trailed off. *Marry me?* Is that what she was really beginning to think? She prayed he wouldn't read her mind because sometimes he came really close.

"If you're waiting for me to apologize for kissing you, I won't." He reached across the empty space between them and grabbed her hands. There was strength and a hardness that matched the calluses on his palms, but his grip was easy.

She told herself she should move away. But she didn't.

"'Aw, come on, Mom, lighten up,' as Jake always says." Matt's grin spread wide, yet it didn't reach his eyes.

She thought of him as being remote and blocked, but was she heading in that direction too? She didn't want to turn into a naggy, hard-edged person just because no one had ever recognized anything of value in her, anything unique about her. That was the one thing setting Matt apart. He had shown from the beginning that he admired her, and he acted as if she was special. Even when he didn't want them here. She could put that down to sexual pull, which she knew they both felt, but it would be sad to think that was the extent of his attraction toward her.

Reluctantly she withdrew her hands from the warmth of his and returned his smile. "I guess I am overprotective. And Jake likes you, too—a lot."

"It's all good. I like him, he likes me, and when you're ready to move on with your life, he will be ready, too. I promise not to hurt him in any way."

You never had a child. How could you know what will hurt? she wanted to ask, but she had no right to judge him. Maybe if a person lives long enough, they learn things about children naturally, even if they have none.

"When do you want us to come to your picnic?" she asked.

"To tell the truth, I'm here for you now."

"You're joking! Now?"

"I'm serious. You said you didn't like things all planned out. I'm practicing being spontaneous."

She laughed. "Nut! You can't practice that."

Looking at him, she knew that if she really tried hard without reservations and didn't hold back because of her own past and her fear of getting hurt again, she might force him to surrender his strangle-hold on *his* past. Was it worth the try?

"Okay," she said. "I'll get the car."

"Uh uh. I brought the mare for you to ride. She's gentle and very pokey. You can sit on her with all the comfort of this big old chair."

"What about Jake?"

"He'll ride with me. I can keep a close watch on him."

"It's too soon after his hospital visit. He's never ridden on a horse before. He's probably allergic to them."

"Hush, Mama Quail. You're all a-twitter again. It'll be fun."

It *did* sound like fun. The only horse she'd ever ridden was as a child on a merry-go-round.

"There's nothing to sitting on a horse. She's old and tame and wouldn't jump if a snake crossed her path. Throw a few things together. Jake and I'll be waiting for you in the front yard." He shoved the chair back and unfolded his long legs. He stopped in the doorway, filling the frame so that he had to tilt his head to look at her. "Got any pie left?"

"Oh, now I get it. You probably wouldn't let me come along with you guys if I didn't have any pie."

His answer was a wide grin and a wink before he closed the screen door behind him.

While she dressed in the bedroom, they came inside. She heard Jake's giggles and the rumble of Matt's low voice as they talked. One part of her wanted this for Jake. So far, only she had been able to make Jake giggle like that.

What should she wear? And why did it matter? She rifled through the closet and took out a turquoise colored shirt and a pair of new jeans. They would be a little tight to begin with. She shouldn't have washed them first. Dressed, she combed her hair, leaving it hang loose.

When she started out of the bedroom, she stopped at the door a moment to watch. Matt sat cross-legged on the floor in front of the fireplace with Jake sprawled at his side. Jake was showing him some of his earlier drawings that he usually put away in a box.

Tears blurred her eyes when Matt patted Jake's head in an awkward but spontaneous gesture of affection. She cleared her throat upon entering the room, to give Matt the time to slide into his laid-back cowboy routine.

Jake managed to talk Matt out of taking time to eat his pie right then, so she loaded it into a bag to carry with her. When Matt told Jake they would ride together, the boy's eyes widened with excitement.

"You named this horse, he'd be put out for sure if you didn't ride him."

Did this man always get his way? He seemed to set things in motion, expecting everything to follow along obligingly. He had that sort of quiet determination bordering on arrogance that both repelled and attracted her. Well, he was in for a surprise if he kept this up. She wasn't the long-suffering pioneer type of woman like his precious Dorothy, content to let some male make all her decisions.

Matt helped her mount the horse—holding her waist a bit longer than necessary, she thought. Tingles flew from his fingers into her body, and she squirmed for fear he would guess the effect he had on her. His big hand lingered on her thigh for a brief moment before he moved toward Jake.

They took off at a slow pace, lulling her earlier apprehensions. "Say, this seems like a round-about way to your house." She heard his laugh even though the back of Jake's hat muffled it.

"We're half-way there now. You're right, we are taking the long way. I wanted to show you and Jake country that you can't see from a truck or car." Matt reined his horse to a stop, waiting for her to catch up. Casey enjoyed riding behind, watching the way they rode together, Jake sitting in front of Matt, holding onto the reins.

She inhaled the sweet smelling pines and watched blue jays squawk as they passed by. "I'm delighted with this route to your house through the pines. Quite a view."

"Nothing like it. Fills a man's soul."

She smiled, willing to bet Jake had the expression of someone whose world had just gotten as good as it would ever get. Matt sat so close to him, his wide shoulders would partially protect her son from the strong sunlight coming down through the tree branches.

Suddenly a scream erupted, bouncing off the canyon walls, reverberating through the trees from the direction of a ledge above the trail.

Casey's horse reared on her hind legs in wild-eyed terror. In a blurred set of motion, Matt leaned forward, grabbing the mare's reins close to the bit, and shouldering up against Casey for support. In a blink of an eye, he reached down toward the scabbard attached to the saddle that held his rifle. He couldn't manage that because of Jake.

His own horse barely flapped his ears, he was so well trained.

"Oh, my God!" Casey cried. "What was that?"

Jake's face blanched, then he looked up at Matt. It twisted something inside Casey to see his eyes so full of trust, watching Matt for a clue as to how he should react.

Matt moved his hands up to hers still holding the reins, though it was no longer necessary. The mare had calmed to a slow walk again.

"That's the puma. He'd never attack, with all of us together." He peered into her face. "You okay?"

"No. Not yet. So much for this horse not getting excited." She surprised herself. She hadn't been that frightened. Not with Matt around.

"First time I've seen her spooked, honest."

She reined the horse past Matt. "I think I'll stay in front, if you don't mind. I don't want any old cat sneaking up on my behind."

"Good idea. I didn't think of that."

"This puma, it wouldn't stray near our cabin, would it? Jake plays in the yard a lot." She didn't want to scare Jake but she needed to know.

"I doubt it. He hangs around the cattle some. I haven't seen any signs of him feeding on any. Birth time is bad, he wouldn't be above grabbing..." As if suddenly remembering Jake's wide-eyed attention, he changed the subject. "Your hands are shaking." He gave a little squeeze to her hands, still cupped around the reins, and moved away.

"Matt! Why didn't you shoot to scare him?" Jake asked, his voice high-pitched with excitement. He took his cue from Matt's quiet composure, and the terror had already left him.

She was very proud of her son. He had the courage and spunk of a boy twice his size.

"I don't bother any critter that leaves me alone," Matt said. "Every animal out here has a purpose."

"What purpose does a...a..." Jake couldn't quite get the words out.

"A puma have? A puma and a mountain lion are the same to us, by the way. As to their purpose, they eat rabbits, gophers, and other pesky varmints. Besides it's enough that they belong here. They are a part of this place just like me. Maybe they don't need an excuse."

She agreed with Matt and felt a surprised admiration for his views. If she had a such a thing as a motto, live and let live would probably be it.

Before turning back to start up the path, Matt adjusted the front rim of his Stetson to shield his eyes as he looked upward. A smile twitched the corners of Casey's mouth when Jake imitated him. Matt winked at her over Jake's head.

The rest of the ride to the ranch was quiet and no one, not even Jake, seemed prone to break the silence.

CHAPTER 11

By the time they arrived at the ranch house, Casey's posterior was so numb she had no feelings except for her inner thighs being hot and sweaty. Not a comfortable sensation. She would probably make a fool of herself by falling down when she tried to walk with legs that felt like sticks of licorice.

They paused at the approach to the ranch. There was no gate, just a cattle guard and an entrance flanked by two giant cottonwoods with the name of the ranch worked in metal suspended from a wrought iron archway.

"TnT?" she asked. She'd noticed it before when she passed through the gate and always wondered what it meant.

Matt pointed up at the sign. "Pop's idea. His name is Thomas and my mother's Theresa. Ending with Tyree, it was a natural. He put a circle around the initials and they call it Circle TnT."

"Good name!" Jake piped up.

Matt flicked the crown of Jake's hat lightly with his fingers. "How are you doing, pard? Bet your legs are asleep by now."

"Well, never mind asking *me*," she grumped. "I'll probably never walk again."

The steady regard in Matt's dark eyes unnerved her. "You did real good on your first ride, especially with the puma making all that racket. Don't worry about your legs and posterior right now," he said. "Tomorrow will be worse. You'll think someone ran over you with a car. It won't last, and after a time or two you'll be old pros at riding."

"I don't think so." Casey stretched, careful not to startle the horse. She still didn't trust it not to run off with her, even if it was a hundred years old. Once she got down on the ground, she wouldn't care if she ever sat on a horse again in spite of his nice compliment.

Not so Jake. She had never seen him so happy. She had worried that he would be allergic to the horses but so far no problem. Of course, with her luck, he would probably break out in hives later.

When they rode into the circular driveway, Carmela came out from inside and Paco ran up from the barn.

Carmela reached her arms up for Jake before anyone could help him down, hugging him briefly as he slipped to the ground. "He feels like a mosquito in my arms. He needs fattening up, with good flour tortillas wrapped around chunks of beef."

Matt bent across the saddle, his lean, hard body causing the leather to squeak in protest, as he touched Casey's shoulder. "He's a fighter. Not many kids would ride all that way without a complaint."

His words of praise made her smile with pleasure. Jake tried to stand taller.

"We heard a puma!" Jake took off his hat and gestured toward the mountains.

Matthew swung his leg out of the saddle. Carmela was still going on about Jake needing more meat on his bones and they all laughed at her, including Paco, who at first seemed embarrassed by her forwardness.

Casey expected Matt to help her down, but after a brief glance in her direction, he began talking to Paco—as if he didn't want to make this day seem like anything but an outing for Jake.

There was no way to deny the attraction between them. Why would he dismiss it, hide his feelings? Surely, this charming couple wouldn't care what his intentions were toward a stranger, would they? Anyway, he didn't strike her as the sort to concern himself about what others thought. So why was he ignoring her now and not helping her off the horse?

Casey slid off the mare. She stretched then rubbed her legs to bring back the circulation. When feeling slowly returned, it was like little needle pricks.

Everyone turned to watch her. "If you don't take us home in your Jeep, I'm walking."

Jake winked at Matt. "She's smiling, but she means it."

"I think one ride a day is enough for a tenderfoot," Matt agreed. "You're doing okay, aren't you?" He knelt on one knee in front of Jake, putting his hands on the boy's shoulders.

Jake nodded. "I liked riding Smokey. It's almost like he's part my horse, 'cause I named him."

Casey watched the interplay between them. This man was an enigma, a bundle of contradictions. One minute he was curt and closed, and the next open and friendly. She hoped she could get Carmela alone and that she would share a little gossip.

"We were lucky this time, but Jake usually has an allergic reaction to animal smells and hair. Not to hurt Smokey's feelings, but he sure smells and he has a lot of hair."

"Next time I'll wash old Smokey down with Lysol before he rides him. How's that? I haven't heard Jake complain." Matt took off his hat and ran his fingers through his hair with an impatient gesture, as if he'd had enough of the conversation.

Lighten up, mother quail, you don't have to wear a chip on your shoulder to keep your balance any more, she scolded herself, hating the defensive way she'd come off just now.

"As a matter of fact," Matt continued. "I think you should get back up on the mare and come with me for a short ride. There's something I want to show you."

She was intrigued, but looked back at the horse she'd just managed to climb off of. "I don't know. I should help in the kitchen..."

Carmela stepped out of the door, as if she'd been listening. "Shoo! I do not need another hand in my kitchen."

Jake grinned up at her. "Go on, Mom. I can help Carmela."

"Paco isn't ready to take out the meat yet," Matt said.

Jake jumped up and down in excitement. "He buries meat in the ground to cook it. I wanna watch him."

"I suppose I could try it, while I'm still numb from the first ride."

Before she could change her mind, Matt led the mare over. She put her foot in the stirrup. "This won't be a long ride, will it?" When he shook his head, she put her leg over and connected with the other stirrup. "Okay, we're ready."

"Don't try to outrun us or gallop ahead," Matt said and laughed back at her as they trotted toward the woods.

She followed behind him. "Hmmph! That's not funny. Me and the old gal have an understanding."

Matthew pointed out different birds that swooped over their heads. Once they caught a glimpse of a porcupine's rear as it waddled away from them.

"If I'm going too fast for you, just let me know," he said and grinned at her over his shoulder.

Casey felt as if his teasing was a bit out of character for him, as if he was trying to keep it light between them. "We could come ahead all right, but it's obvious there's not enough room to ride side by side."

Abruptly he stopped and waited for her. His smile told her he wanted to make another observation about her speed on the horse but refrained. A clearing lay just ahead as they topped the rise together. She gasped. Below, in a picturesque meadow, deer stood placidly munching on grass. Two young ones drank at a nearby pond. The scene was so peaceful that neither Casey or Matt broke the silence.

When his horse grew restive and snorted, the deer raised their heads and looked in their direction. Matt nodded to her and they turned their horses back before they could spook the deer.

"That was beautiful. Apparently you don't hunt or they would be more cautious."

"We used to, Pop and I. But it seemed pointless to turn something so splendid into meat when we had cattle that are born and raised for that purpose. So one year we both decided to let it be."

His dark lashes hid his eyes before he turned away as if his feelings weren't manly. But his father apparently felt the same. This was a side to him that appealed to her—a man who could live the life of a rancher and yet have feelings toward animals.

"Race you to the house," he yelled back as he kneed his horse forward. His laughter rang out through the woods and she shook the reins of the bridle urging the mare into at least a mild trot. There had to be a way to get back at him. When she saw what looked like a side trail that led up a hill in the direction they had just come back from, an idea formed. She almost laughed out loud. Perfect. She'd make sure they came back here another day to make the plan work.

They entered the yard of the house and Jake was waiting to greet them. "Mmm. I smell something good," Casey said.

As they dismounted, a big, yellow blur came from behind the house and leaped toward Matt and Jake.

He turned and knelt to caress the head of a large, shaggy animal. "Some damn fool dropped her off in the woods and she turned up here. She's probably part lab and part collie and she has pups. Want to see them, Jake?"

Oh boy, next thing he would have Jake wanting a puppy.

She reached down to pet the dog and looked toward the house.

The wide veranda encircling the entire house appealed to her. It would be nice screened in. Maybe no one ever thought of that idea.

"Pop built it when he first bought the property. He and Paco did it together. We've added to it over the years."

For some reason Casey wanted to know if Dorothy had lived here before they built their own home. She also knew it was a touchy subject, so she didn't ask. But he seemed to zone in on her thoughts.

"Pop and I built my house. Then I brought Dorothy to the ranch. She would never have moved here to the big house though, she liked her own place."

"Where is that?" Casey asked. It came as a surprise that he was willing to talk of Dorothy. It was probably a good thing for him to open up about it.

"Over that way, just the other side of the corral, beyond that grove of trees." He pointed toward a small dirt road that curled into the distance between a grove of trees.

"Come in, come in," Carmela had disappeared for a few minutes and emerged now on the porch to beckon them. Her round form preceded them into the house while Matthew held open the door.

Just inside the doorway, Casey paused, blinking at the sudden absence of sunlight. Jake held tight to her hand, but when Matt glanced their way, he quickly let go.

When her eyes adjusted to the dimness, she looked around. It was a homey room, with a step down center and a huge fireplace. Indian rugs hung on the knotty pine walls and through the colorful rugs scattered on the floor she saw large squares of terrazzo tiles in muted shades of brown and sage green. Trophies stood on a sideboard and when she looked in that direction, Matt grinned.

Matt regarded her with a steady gaze; as if he hoped she liked the room. "My dad was proud of our ranch. We used to breed, raise, and show quarter horses. Mom forbade me to get rid of anything in this room until they came back."

She pointed toward a wall of books. "It's a lovely room. Someone must read a lot."

"I brought most of them over from my house. But yes, I do read a lot. Does that surprise you?"

"I don't exactly regard you as a Neanderthal." She couldn't resist a taunting little flick of her tongue across her lips.

The gesture wasn't lost on him, as the side of his mouth twitched in amusement. "Exactly?"

She looked at Jake and Carmela who were taking in their conversation with apparent relish. "Maybe we should move along," she suggested.

"Go ahead, Carmela, show them around." Matt turned away to the roll top desk in a corner, and brought the door down on a stack of wrinkled papers that appeared vaguely familiar to Casey.

He motioned to Jake. "Come on, let's get some fresh air and let these women yak." In the kitchen, Casey stopped to admire the spacious room. It had a brick fireplace, large enough to walk upright inside. A tall, antique rocker sat on a round hooked rug in front of a brick wall holding shiny copper pots and pans. More copper and cast iron pans hung behind the two stoves. Windows let in light and looked out on the porch.

"Why are there two of everything?" Casey asked. There were two refrigerators, two freezers, and two stoves.

"When Matthew's mother and father lived here, we fed the crew in the bunkhouse. Always a crowd around the place. It was better then, not so quiet. Now at spring roundup, Matthew's father comes to join him and they hire a few men from town. They don't let Paco do much, he's getting to be an old man." She laughed uproariously at her private joke.

Casey guessed the man and wife were nearly the same age.

Carmela poured two cups of coffee and motioned Casey to follow through the kitchen door out to the veranda where they sat on rockers. The view was spectacular. Casey inhaled the clean air and looked out over the forest in the distance and the mountains beyond. The sky was a brilliant blue without a cloud in sight. Such a mixed up land, part high desert with dry brown weeds, part evergreen forest and always the mountains. It must be magnificent in the winter.

Carmela placed a brown, plump hand on Casey's arm. "Do not give up on Matthew. You don't give up on your son. It is the same."

Casey hid her surprise at Carmela jumping right in with personal talk. "Matt is hurting, but he's grown accustomed to it after all these years. He uses the hurt for comfort and to protect himself."

Carmela had a little sad smile on her lips. "That is true. You are wise to see it. He must put the past aside. You can help him."

Casey shook her head. "Oh no. I can't help him. We barely know each other."

"But you *can*! The heart is not concerned with time. I saw the way you looked at each other. Something is growing between you. Allow it to strength and blossom. Someone must give enough to begin. He won't, ever."

Thinking about Carmela's words, Casey rocked gently. No denying the attraction between her and Matt. Part of it could be his compassion for Jake. Being a rancher, he no doubt felt the same protectiveness toward any helpless creature. He was probably more at home with a dependent creature, which would leave him in control, keeping his defensive coating of toughness intact.

"There is something which has already made a difference. Maybe I should not speak of it." Carmela's voice was subdued, as if the men out in the yard could hear her.

"What is it?" Casey asked.

"You noticed the pile of little papers on his desk before he closed it?"

"Yes. Only because he shut the cover so fast, as if he didn't want us to see something."

Carmela said, "This is truly so. He has been collecting pieces of paper with poetry written on them. He hasn't shown them to anyone, but I am cursed with a terrible curiosity." She rolled her eyes and shrugged as if to say, what's a person to do? "I had to read one."

Casey flushed, thinking of her heart and soul poured into the anonymous notes. Had he figured out who wrote them? She didn't think so, since he had seemed so direct, he probably would have mentioned them before this. On the other hand, why try to hide them?

"I held one of the papers in my hand and saw a vision of your hair, like an explosion of fire in the sunlight. When you came here that night with your sick boy, I was very sure you wrote them."

"Yes. I did. When we first moved here it was a very lonely time for me. I needed someone to talk to, but didn't think anyone would read my poems. I don't want Matt to know they are mine—if he doesn't know already."

"The smartest man can be very slow at times. He has it in his head they are from a village over the range of hills. Something to do with the wind currents. Men are so foolish."

"I would never describe him as foolish. He is obviously a practical person."

"Do you see how you are reaching out? You can help him. He can help you. You need each other."

Casey smiled gently, touching Carmela's clasped hands. "That's the problem. I don't *want* to help him. It sounds selfish, but concentrating on Jake is giving me enough to worry about. I just ended a relationship where he had all his needs met and mine got ignored. I won't fall into that trap again."

Carmela tsk tsked, looking as if she did not believe a word Casey said.

The moment Casey spoke the words, their hypocrisy rattled against her conscience. It was possible to devise all kinds of negative thoughts, but impossible to deceive herself. She *did* want to help Matt, but it seemed so hopeless. He is shut down tight, holding on to his memories for dear life. How can you read a closed book?

"One page at a time," Carmela said quietly.

Casey jumped. How spooky! She hadn't said a word out loud but Carmela had apparently been eavesdropping on her thoughts. Casey rubbed the goose bumps from her arms and changed the subject abruptly, as she usually did when she felt uncomfortable.

"You've been with Matt since he was born?"

Carmela rocked in short little strokes. Everything about her was short and round and soft. "*Sí.* Senor Thomas had this house built for his new wife. Paco helped. When they settled in, Paco returned to Mexico and found me in a little mountain village. He said he searched all Mexico for the right woman." Her strong voice rose a notch in pride. "I tell him I was the only one who would go with him." She giggled.

"And just like that, you left your family to come here with him? To a strange land—to live among strangers?"

"I had no family. I lived with an aunt, as old as the river that ran behind our house. She never wanted the bother of a girl to care for. When my mother died she took me in because the church told her to."

That was uncanny. As if Carmela's life mirrored her own.

"Did you and Paco have children? You're probably a great-grandmother by now."

Carmela's face looked bleak for a brief moment before she recovered. "We had a son. We raised him along with Matthew. He was riding in the back of the truck when Dorothy and her unborn son died. They all died. Except Matthew. For that he will never forgive himself. He is a tortured with a terrible guilt that will not leave him."

"Oh, I'm so sorry. I didn't know about your son. Matt hinted of an accident that killed his wife. His mother mentioned it too. But truly, I didn't know about your son."

"It is a miracle he even mentioned the accident to you. He never speaks of it. He even spoke Dorothy's name today, of that I am surprised."

"I know he didn't want to go into details but he did say a few words about her dying in an accident."

Carmela rolled her eyes upward and crossed herself. "That is a sign. A true sign from the angels. He has never spoken of this terrible time to anyone, not even his mother and father. He feels he is to blame, we all know that, but can do nothing. At first, we told him so many times we did not blame him for Manuel's death. Now no one dares speak of it."

"How it must have hurt to lose your only son."

"It grows easier with time. I do not keep a shrine for him as Matthew does for his wife. Sometimes I tell Paco, he should burn that house down to the ground. It is filled with spirits who do not wish to remain on earth. Matthew is keeping his wife and unborn son here, against their will."

Shivers ran up Casey's spine and the hair on her arms stirred at the picture Carmela's words painted.

"When Matthew accepts that his first family is dead and gone, and that it was not anything he could have prevented, he will also accept that we never blamed him for our son's death either. I pray for that day before he throws away his life. What a terrible waste that would be."

They sat for a few moments, both overwhelmed by the conversation.

Finally Carmela spoke. "Forgive me. I am an old woman with too much time on her hands. I pray Senor Thomas and Theresa return someday. They would, if their son ever loses this obsession. That is why they moved to town, to get Matthew out of the other house and into this one."

"You must be really close to Mr. and Mrs. Tyree."

"Theresa is like a sister to me. She never treated me as a servant and insists I call her by her name. I miss her. There was so much joy and laughter when they were here. I think it is a wrong thing they do. They are not helping Matthew by leaving him alone. Except he did finally move out of his house into this one, which is better."

"He won't let anyone into his heart."

Carmela shook her head vehemently. "He has allowed your son inside."

"Yes, he and Jake have formed a bond, I guess. Perhaps because Matt feels protective."

"It is a first step."

"I'm sorry. I recognize your feelings for Matt. He must be like a son to you. But don't put this on my shoulders. I don't have the time or energy to give him. I'm trying to get over my own personal disaster and my son has to come first."

"That is not altogether true anymore. You have given yourself permission to end a connection that was not good for you and now it is past. *You* must come first. For without you, there would be no son, either in the beginning or now."

"How do you know these things?"

Carmela smiled. "In Mexico I was a *curandera*, a healer. Some called me *bruja*, sorcerer. I see things. Things I wish not to see sometimes."

"Why not? Isn't your gift helpful to others?"

"Not always. Sometimes it is a painful burden, when you see happenings which you are helpless to prevent or change."

"Did you see—did you know about the accident before it happened?"

Carmela nodded and turned her head away.

Casey knew the dark eyes filled with tears. She put her hand gently on Carmela's shoulder.

"I did not see it until Matthew and my son had left. Paco and I jumped in the old truck to try and stop them, but when we got to the crossing, it was too late."

"Does Matthew know this?"

"I told him, a long time after." She folded her apron in tiny pleats with nervous fingers. "That is the only time I've ever feared Matthew, when I tried to tell him what I saw. He was like a wild man, cursing and shouting. I think part of him believed me, that the accident could have been prevented if we had reached that place sooner. Life does not work in that manner. We are set on our paths and it was their time to leave the earth. We've never spoken of it since."

Just then, Jake ran up on the porch, shattering the emotional tension between the two women.

CHAPTER 12

"Mom! Paco is making a huge fire and we're going to eat ribs. Barbecue ribs!"

"You know better than that, son. You can't eat meat until the doctors say it's okay."

"Why not? How much can he eat?" Matt cleared the steps in two strides and stood by Jake, his hand resting on the boy's shoulder.

A twinge of irritation fought with the quick exhilaration that Matthew's presence brought her. "Some of the doctors think too much protein in his diet may be counter-productive in overcoming his allergies." She listened to herself and knew she had to overcome this fierce protectiveness. Jake was doing okay now.

"Beef, that's what he needs. Everyone thrives on beef." Matt clenched his fist to make an exaggerated muscle, straining the material on his arm and sounding caveman grunts, causing Jake to laugh.

She couldn't help but smile. "You sound like a television commercial."

"Come on with me. Carmela's beat your ear long enough. I want to show you and Jake the corral and the horses." He reached for her hand.

"Let's go, Mom." Jake took her other hand to pull her up from the chair. Casey shot a look in Carmela's direction, seeing the knowing smile on her plump face.

"You go. Shush now." Carmela made a shooing gesture with her apron. "I'll finish the potato salad and boil the corn on the cob."

"I'd like to help," Casey offered, hoping she wouldn't take her up on it.

"You're a terrible cook. Let Carmela do it." Jake stood looking up at her, tugging at her hand.

"Oh she is, is she?" Matt laughed at Casey's embarrassment. "Maybe she'll have to come by for lessons from Carmela."

"Good idea," Jake said. "She bakes good pies and cookies though," he conceded.

"Okay, you two, never mind deciding my future. As it happens, I don't *like* to cook."

"Harumph!" Jake snorted. "Richard never liked you to."

Casey paused on her way out the door to point her finger at Jake. He knew she didn't like him calling his father Richard. This was the first time in weeks he spoke of his father and in such a matter-of-fact way. Was he getting over the divorce and the loss of one parent? That shouldn't be too hard for him, given he'd never had a real father in the first place. Casey felt guiltier over what they had put Jake through with their quarrels than she did of depriving him of a father's physical presence. And Jake had used an expression straight from the Colonel and didn't realize it, how funny.

Matthew came close and bent his head to peer into her eyes. "Penny for your thoughts."

"They aren't worth it," she countered lightly.

"You've got eyes the color of a Colorado sky," he said.

Casey had a hard time pulling her gaze away. Her lips felt on fire, so close, so close to his. She edged away, breaking the spell "Thank you. It's a beautiful sky."

"That's what's so great about Colorado. Pop came here on a cattle drive and fell for the country. My mother came from the city. He likes to tell the story of how he went to Center City, met her, courted her, and two weeks later they were married. He brought her back here and to hear him tell it, she came directly from pioneering stock, took to the ranch like a duck to water."

Casey liked the way he gradually opened up with conversation now. It was as if he normally cast himself in the mold of a taciturn cowboy and had begun to realize that a little social interaction was not a bad thing. At least she hoped she was reading him right.

"Matthew's feet are down into tap roots by now. He will never leave here, any more than me or Carmela." Paco stood just outside the porch, at the bottom of the steps, waiting for them.

"The folks left, didn't they?" Matt countered.

"Someday they will return. Carmela says so."

Matt reached for Jake's hand and Casey's elbow, steering them down the porch steps. His light grasp made her skin tingle, and her crazy heart flutter. For a moment, she felt giddy and lightheaded. Caution bells sent reverberations through her head as she struggled to fight the need his contact stirred within.

"I'd like...I wonder if you could show us around the ranch, you know, drive down that way a bit. It looks interesting down by those big trees where your house is. You mentioned a pond."

Carmela's indrawn breath behind them was the first indication that she had said the wrong thing. The second was Matt's frown. A sudden silence spread around them like fog creeping in from the ocean.

"No."

She was getting to really dislike those monosyllables of his. They were at once charming, sexy, and irksome. Even Jake noticed it and was doing it to her sometimes.

"What about the eagle nest? Wouldn't that be a good thing to show them?" Paco asked quietly.

Jake reached up and took Matt's hand, shaking it lightly to get his attention." Come on, Matt, please? I'd like to see an eagle."

Bless Jake and Paco, she thought as Matthew tore his gaze from hers and looked down at the boy. She held her breath. She had never been able to refuse her son anything when he coaxed her with those round blue eyes, too big for his face.

Matt relented, his rugged features easing into an embarrassed expression. "It's my—our old house down there. No reason you'd want to see it, but I guess it wouldn't hurt. There are swings in the trees too."

He had made a swing for his unborn child, how sad. Now Casey wasn't sure she wanted to go there, but Matt opened the Jeep door, expecting them to get in. She spared a quick glimpse at the couple standing on the porch. Paco's countenance showed puzzlement, as if he couldn't believe his eyes, but Carmela had a smug expression on her face. She wasn't surprised. She had known this would happen.

Jake prattled on while they jounced down the road. It was overgrown with weeds pushing in from the sides and ruts from the last rains, obviously seldom used. Sometimes in the sunlight, she caught sight of cobwebs strung across the trail from tree to tree.

Matt turned into the yard and braked the car, sitting still while Jake opened the back door and leaped out.

"Mom! Look! Swings!" He ran toward the trees where two tires swung by stout ropes, as well as a sedate swing hanging by chains from a large tree.

Casey imagined Matt and his wife planning children with such faith and love. It made her hesitate to intrude, and yet she sensed this was the core to Matt's bitterness and isolation. It was like a boil needing to be lanced. "If you'd rather not—" she began.

"We're here, aren't we?"

She wasn't put off by his shortness this time, knowing how much he hurt. He couldn't have visited here for a long time, judging from the old leaves and broken branches in the rutted road leading to the house. She followed him up the steps with Jake close behind. Matt pushed open the unlocked door, stepping back for them to enter.

Once inside Jake started sneezing.

"There's an inch of dust covering everything." Matt's deep voice was hushed as if he hated to disturb anything, even the air. "Carmela refuses to come here, says the house has ghosts."

"Jake, honey, you go outside and play on the swings." He didn't have to be here with the dust.

"In a second, Mom," he said.

Matt stepped away to gaze out the front window, leaving her to walk around. At first, she felt like a trespasser in another woman's home, looking at her private possessions without permission.

"Wow! It's like a museum!" Jake exclaimed. Even he was subdued, trying to step on top of Matt's bootsteps so as not to so as not to make extra shoe prints in the dust on the floor.

She didn't miss the little tug of wry humor at the edge of Matt's lips when he turned to watch them.

The couches and tables in the front room had been covered by sheets, which made the house seem more eerie than it should have. "Jake, mind me now. You'd better skedaddle if you want to stay for the picnic. You're going to get all choked up." Casey had the feeling of smothering, as if the air had been sucked dry from the room, leaving only dust motes floating toward the windows.

She stood in the middle of the room, turned away from Jake and Matt while they talked in low tones. She closed her eyes. "Dorothy, if you are here, let him go," she whispered softly.

Casey waited, holding her breath. A feeling of peace settled around her shoulders and engulfed her body. Her scalp crinkled with a cold shiver. That was when she knew what Carmela said was true. Dorothy wasn't holding on to Matt. It was Matt who wouldn't let go.

Right at this moment, she realized how much she had come to care for Matt and how bereft she and Jake would be if they never saw him again. Was she falling in love?

Impossible!

He was nothing like the man she wanted to spend the rest of her life with. He was rigid in his beliefs, centered here on this ranch, and he didn't have a romantic hair on his head. Oh no, she was not about to fall in love with him. She just craved his friendship. Yeah, that was it.

"Ready?" His gruff voice broke into her thoughts and as she turned to go, she felt a sigh of air sifting over her like a soft summer rain. It was as if Dorothy had said goodbye.

Outside, Jake sneezed a few more times and then pronounced himself okay. They laughed and Matthew beckoned to them. "Walk with me back to the pond. I want to show you something."

They walked through the narrow trail downward to a clearing past a cluster of trees. "The pond's not big anymore," Matt said. "Pop stocked it with catfish at one time and there are probably some big ones left. He keeps threatening to come back here and fish them out."

Matt put out his arm to hold them back. "There. See that lightning-struck tree? "He pointed toward a blackened, barkless tree standing by itself in the midst of a meadow. "We call it Old Lonesome. If you look way up at the top, you can spot the eagle's nest. I wanted Jake to watch the female, she comes back and forth, feeding her brood. Biggest specimen ever seen in these parts." He handed over the binoculars he brought from the car.

While Jake searched for the large bird, Matt and Casey sat on a rustic bench, carved from a log. It was a while before either of them spoke.

"This is a lovely spot," she finally said to break the silence.

"Sure was—is. At first, I used to drive over here and sit a lot. I didn't like the worry that my coming here caused the folks so I quit. After they left I was out of the habit."

"It would be hard to let go. You have beautiful memories. When you split up with someone you once loved, for whatever reasons, you have nothing left. The memories are all tainted."

When he looked into her eyes, she had the strong sensation of sinking in a sea of warm brown pain. She couldn't bear it and turned away.

"You have Jake."

"Yes. I have Jake."

They didn't speak for a few more minutes and then she said, "It has to be hard to let someone go. Someone you loved so fiercely."

Matt didn't answer. He rose and took the binoculars from Jake. She rose as well, and they gradually walked back up the trail. Every so often Jake ran to explore a toadstool or exclaim at seeing a squirrel scurry up a tree. Once he brought Casey a wild flower he plucked from a group nestled at the base of a tree.

"I hope you don't care that I picked it for mom." He looked up at Matt, who shook his head.

Casey tucked the flower in a buttonhole, and they sat on another bench while Jake swung from the tire.

"Fiercely?" Matt finally said. "That's a strange word. I never thought of it that way. Dot and I knew each other since high school and always knew we would marry. There never was anyone else for either of us."

She waited, thinking there might be more he wanted to say. When he didn't speak, she said, "Well, you did go out on dates first and courted her, brought her flowers sometimes, that's a plus."

"Didn't have to. She wanted to be married and start a home, and we were both ready." His tone of voice said that was the end of it.

She couldn't let it go. "Every woman needs courting. She needs to know she is loved—to be offered little surprises like an occasional bouquet of flowers or a love note, just some thought and special consideration. The practical can come later, but the other makes a basis for the rest of a couple's life together."

He turned his body toward her on the bench and looked so steadily at her that it was unnerving. Her words had sounded shallow and inane even to her own ears, but she jutted out her chin just the same. She might not have used the right words, but he had to know what she meant.

"There's a saying, 'she's a woman to ride the river with.' Out here that's the kind of partner you need. A man isn't looking for a hothouse flower that will fade away with the first hard times. Because there's plenty of that here. Some years we have drought and you end up shooting your cattle if you can't sell them, just to put them out of their misery. A prairie fire can sweep through and you spend your next two years of profit feeding the cattle with bought hay."

Here she was, rattling on about looking for a knight in shining armor, and he could only see the heavy loads in life. Couldn't the two ideas exist together? Didn't the hard life need a little softening of fantasy and romance?

Not to him, apparently. "Your parents are enjoying themselves traveling. There are other things in life besides work."

"I suppose Pop likes moving around, or he wouldn't do it. They go to square dances in town when they stay here. Last time we talked, they were learning line dancing, of all things. Sounds nonsensical to me."

Pity. He had all the possibilities of a good dancer. He moved with a grace that belied his size. "Haven't you ever liked to dance?" She asked.

"I don't see the point."

"Does everything have to have a point? There isn't much point in tennis, or swimming, or playing Scrabble. It's a way to pass time, to share and enjoy life."

"I don't see those things as enjoyment."

Casey persisted, telling herself all along that it was like talking to a brick wall. "Dancing is something couples do. To come together. It's romantic."

He settled his arms across his chest and looked her straight in the eye. "Romantic! Who has time for that nonsense?" When she didn't answer, he continued. "Living in a cabin in the woods might seem appealing to someone from the city. Still, the solar panels don't work with snow covering them, sometimes the fireplace clogs up and you wouldn't have heat. I'm gone a lot during the winter, looking for strays. You, for example, couldn't stay in the cabin alone."

It always comes back to her and Jake leaving. Her first impulse was exasperation. How would he know where they could stay? She didn't belong anywhere and the notion made her voice snappish. "How do you set yourself up to judge who does or does not belong here? I know it's your property, but—"

"I'm just talking about survival, I'm not judging anything. There is a generator for emergencies and an underground line from the main house to the cabin. But you can't turn on two appliances at the same time. With the little refrigerator, that's about it. The cooking stove runs on propane and there's a big tank out back, so you'd not likely run out, even with a lot of baking, but even propane lines freeze up some winters."

"I guess that pretty well sums it up. You don't have to go on."

His lips turned up in a barely perceptible grin. "We have an artesian well and the water's piped down so that's not a worry, but we shut it off to the cabin in the winter to avoid breaking lines."

Casey felt touched by his isolation, as if he had to prove he didn't need anyone. At the same time, she was angry with him constantly trying to get rid of her and Jake. He was as committed Dorothy as if she were still alive. He would never change, never bend. Forget what Carmela said, forget what Casey's own senses tried to impart. Matthew was an empty shell with nothing left inside.

She wasn't much better off, having spent her energy getting away on her own and fighting for the right to take care of Jake. That didn't allow much of anything left over for anyone else in her life either. Yet, her emotions as well as her body craved fulfillment. She felt his strength, his goodness, his loyalty, even while she recognized his faults—the single-mindedness, his stubborn, hardheaded way of bullying right through to what he wanted.

But his most damning flaw was the closed reserve she saw in him at times. It was a barrier to any free and giving relationship, even if she had entertained the idea briefly. She was a romantic at heart, and he lacked a romantic soul.

That, to her, was insurmountable.

CHAPTER 13

When they pulled up in front of the main house, Jake jumped out, hitting the ground at a run to tell Carmela all he had seen. They had become instant friends, and it pleased Casey. Every child should have a grandmotherly figure in his life and so far, Jake didn't have that. She was also happy to realize that she no longer felt possessive and jealous when others came into Jake's life.

The big dog raced toward Jake. He grabbed the animal by the thick ruff of hair on his neck. Casey smiled, holding herself in check. *He's going to be okay, leave it alone.*

Carmela called out to Casey and gave her the task of bringing trays of food to the wooden picnic tables under the big oak tree in the front yard.

"Come on, Jake, I want you to see something behind the house." Matt put his hand on Jake's shoulder and they disappeared around the corner.

Not many minutes passed before they returned, with Jake holding a puppy. "Look, Mom, Sunny had babies." He ran to show her.

Casey couldn't bear to rain on his parade, he was so excited. "That's a beauty. Be careful not to squeeze it." She looked up at Matt, whose eyes glinted with mischief. He knew Jake would be enthralled. "Thought you didn't name animals," she said. "You named the mother dog."

"Nope. Jake named her. He said her fur looked like it was full of sun."

"Well, guess that's pretty darned appropriate. Now how about putting it back? Sunny is looking anxious and we are ready to eat almost. And don't forget to wash your hands."

When Matt and Jake came back, they sat down to a brimming table heaped with iced tea, lemonade, a huge platter of fresh corn on the cob, beef ribs that could have come from a dinosaur, and large bowls of coleslaw and potato salad. There was also a chocolate cake that made Jake's eyes light up.

"I'm sorry *someone* didn't give me enough notice to bring more pies," Casey said, looking at Matt.

"Hey, I said I was practicing being spontaneous, didn't I?"

"She bakes good pies and cookies," Jake chimed in.

"I'll say. Carmela, you're the best cook going, but you have to taste one of her gigantic Jake cookies." Matt made a circle holding his two hands up, with fingers spread to meet his thumbs.

"Ha, did you hear that, Mom? Jake cookies."

"Yes, I heard. And thank you, Matt, for the compliment." She might float off up into the trees with all the love and camaraderie felt around the table. Oh, this was so good for Jake.

She watched her son eat prodigious amounts of food, his face smeared from cheek to cheek with barbecue sauce. Never once did she remind him to use his napkin. The conversation buzzed around her, with Matt talking more than he usually did, and Paco jamming his words in, squeezing them between Carmela's chatting.

"Oh boy, I'm getting full," Casey finally said, putting down her fork. "Everything's so good. I don't remember when I ate so much and enjoyed it so."

Carmela looked at her and smiled. "You and Jake both need to put meat on your bones. Food is for the soul as much as for the body."

"Watch out, she'll have you so round you won't be able to wobble up the front steps," Matt said.

Paco laughed. "He's right. She will stuff you like a goose. It's a challenge to her."

"You don't see Matthew or Paco heavy, do you?" Carmela said. "It's a matter of eating food you enjoy with good company." She patted her tummy and smiled. "I do not say the same for myself, but I blame my ancestors, who, I am told were all round and short."

"Okay, I believe you, Carmela, but I might have to remind you of that someday when you have to roll me up a hill to get me here." The words started out flippant but ended up sad because they reminded Casey that she might not be here that long.

Jake excused himself and ran to play on the lawn with the dog. What next, skydiving? Bungee jumping? But setting aside control felt good for a change. Carmela waved her away and she and Paco began clearing off the table. Matt and Casey took their coffee and went to sit under a big cottonwood tree.

When they settled, Matt reached for her hand and held it. "I don't want to pound it into the ground, but you can't spend the winter here alone, you must know that."

His quiet, steady voice penetrated her thoughts, sending ripples of awareness through her body as she absorbed his words.

"The clean, dry air has been good for Jake."

He took his hand away and stared down at his boots, the silence extending between them. In the background, she could hear Carmela talking away to Paco and Jake giggling with the dog. She watched shards of sunlight play on the thickest part of Matt's hair. He wore it fairly short, but then she couldn't imagine him ever having it shoulder length like most of the boys she grew up with. The slight whisper of gray edging just above his ears gave him a distinguished appearance, which his mischievous grin immediately destroyed.

"You're going to get your hackles up when I say this, but I don't like wasted words. I am one to speak my mind. You think it may be the sunlight, the air that's helping Jake. It may be that you're *letting* him live. Gradually coming to see him as a person, not a possession which you could lose any time and must protect at all costs."

Her first reaction was defensive. "That's baloney. Possession? I act like Jake is a possession? Of course I protect him. You've no idea how many times I almost lost him."

"You're so easy-going, so up-beat about everything else. I can't see you as the smother-mother type. Just give him room to breathe."

"First I have to make sure he's able to."

"And that's what I'm saying. There's no doubt it's been a good experience for him up here. Come back in the spring and the place is yours again."

He wouldn't miss her. She turned away, not wanting him to look into her eyes. He touched her chin with his thumb and turned her back to face him.

"I don't want you to go. But I can't say it strongly enough to get through to you. Sometimes we get a mild winter, but most are colder than you could imagine. I remember one winter when I was a kid, and the snow came down in a continual blizzard that lasted for weeks. There wasn't a rancher in the state who didn't lose cattle. We'd have lost ours too, but Pop found an old mining tunnel not far away. We drove them inside for protection and brought them hay and water."

"I would think cattle can stand a lot of cold."

"They can. But when the snow's so deep, they breathe in the cold, which coats their lungs. They get pneumonia and just stand there, dying on their feet."

"That's pitiful."

"You're damned right it is, but a rancher can't afford to let emotions get to him. You have to see animals as machines or you wouldn't survive. When you put a sick one down, when you castrate the young ones at spring roundup, when you have to sew up tears and cuts or help with a breech birth. It's part of the business."

"Is that why you wouldn't name your horse?"

"That's part of it."

"Then why didn't you hunt down the puma?"

"I may have to yet, if he gets bolder. I won't hesitate if it becomes necessary. Most of the big cats move off, go higher where the rabbits and deer are plentiful. I wouldn't shoot anything in front of Jake, for sure."

Casey felt her eyes mist at his unexpected mixture of hardness and compassion.

His dark brows drew into a frown. "Promise me you'll think it over, about winter. I can't force you to leave, that would be awkward, but I'm only thinking of you both."

And probably don't want us as another responsibility. In spite of the cynical trend of her thoughts, she understood where he was coming from, because there could be no doubt that Jake had gotten under his skin, past his protective armor.

"I will think about it. *When* I must leave, I mean. Carmela says your parents might come back before winter."

"Carmela imagines she sees things. Yet, it could happen. They have the little house in Parker to stay in. They might continue traveling. But they did mention staying in Dorothy's house, if they decided to come back to the ranch."

Dorothy's house. He couldn't let that go. "Wouldn't they stay in the main house with you?"

He shook his head, his strong, sun browned features softened as his mouth spread in a sardonic grin. "I doubt it. One of my mother's pet sayings is, 'there's no house big enough for two families.'"

"But you're not a..."

"Not a family? Is that what you were going to say?" He got up from the chair and moved away, leaning against the tree trunk. "No, I guess I'm not a family."

Casey was sorry the moment her words popped out of her mouth. Now they hung in the air between them. "I just meant that even without Dorothy, you are still separate, not really a part of your parent's life since you became an adult. That's a normal situation, isn't it?"

"I suppose. I overhead Carmela tell Paco that the folks were depressed by my moping. Can you imagine that? I didn't even know a grown man *could* mope. That may be why they won't stay with me in the main house."

It seemed to Casey that this was the first time he admitted the truth, that Carmela might have been right and his parents did feel that way. It was sad, but understandable. Besides, a grown man could mope. However, she wasn't about to lay that on him.

She stood up to stretch, rubbing her backside. "I think it's time Jake and I went back to the cabin. I'll go find Carmela and Paco and thank them."

"Okay, I'll wait by the Jeep. That is if you're sure you don't want to ride back on the horses. Won't take me a minute to saddle up."

Oh, that wondrous roguish grin. "No, thanks. Remember you said one ride would be enough for one day?"

Once inside, Carmela wasn't ready to let her go without a few last words. "Come, I want to show you something."

Casey followed her outside where the older woman knelt to clip pieces of green from little bushes. Carmela handed her a piece to smell and taste.

"Mmm. Mint."

Carmela smiled. "*Sí. Yerba buena.* Make a mild tea to give to your son twice a day. It will calm his nerves, open his sinus." She reached for a garden spade and dug up a batch with roots, which she put into a nearby container. "Plant this in your yard. If you go, take some with you. Only, *mihija,* my daughter, I do not think you will go."

"Matt said the winters could get rough. I don't have a telephone and the cabin isn't insulated enough to keep warm. Plain and simple, he doesn't want us here."

Carmela only smiled and shook her head, handing Casey the planter filled with mint.

She hugged Carmela and shook hands with Paco. On the way home, Jake lay in the back seat, almost asleep. Odd how it felt like a family, the three of them in Matt's car, bumping down the narrow lane. She closed her eyes against the sudden thrust of loneliness.

During the following week, Jake seemed unusually subdued. He drew several pictures to put in the tumbleweeds, but since Matt knew about the poems, she couldn't think of anything to write. Even if he didn't know for sure where they came from, the idea of him reading them was inhibiting. Eventually he would find out the truth. Jake would most likely let it slip, since he could never keep a secret.

"You okay, sweetie?" She asked him one morning, a few days after the barbecue.

"Sure, Mom." He smiled. He took on a little more color every day and the night sweats had nearly stopped.

"Maybe we should take a trip to Center City, see Dr. Watson this week. It wouldn't hurt. Dr. Watson was Jake's pediatrician in Phoenix and had notified her that he was relocating in Center City, Colorado. That had been one reason she thought it a good idea to come here.

"Aw, you worry too much. I'm fine, honest. I liked Dr. Watson but I already went to doctors in Parker."

He had never spoken of his trip to the hospital or the visit from his grandparents and it was just as well.

If only she could be sure the Nichols wouldn't intrude into their lives again. Next time they might bring Richard. She was not the same person who left him, but she wasn't sure she was ready to face him. Not yet.

CHAPTER 14

Casey had been lost in the editing of her book, unaware of the passing time, when Jake's shout from outside shot her to her feet. She bolted for the door, wondering what was wrong. Having a hard time calming her crazy heart, she swallowed when she recognized Matt pulling up in the Jeep.

Jake ran forward. When Matt got down, it seemed for a moment that he didn't know what to do with Jake and then he lifted him and swung him above his head. Jake laughed, his hands on Matt's shoulders.

Roughhousing was good for Jake. It was hard being all-things to a boy. As a single parent, she had a lot to learn and was learning through trial and error. Knowing Jake would probably not have a normal set of grandparents made her sad.

Casey walked down the steps to greet Matt. She immediately noticed how bright and fresh the day had turned and sniffed appreciatively of the pine smell. The sun felt good on her body and warmed her from the inside out. She and Jake should get outside more before winter.

She smiled at Matt. "Hi. Come on in for a cup of coffee. Maybe I could locate some Jake cookies."

For a moment he studied her intently, his brown eyes unfathomable. Then for a heart-stopping moment, she saw a vulnerable, naked yearning in his eyes.

"Your hair—it's like a halo of fire around your head," he said.

"That's very poetic for a he-man rancher," she answered lightly, moved to the point that she couldn't say anymore. Jake ran ahead up the stairs and they followed.

He grinned. "I don't have a poetic bone in my body. Never had time. Day-dreaming is for people with too much time on their hands."

"Ah, you don't mean that. Everyone needs a dream now and again." She felt Matt's eyes on her back as she turned and went through the door ahead of him. She knew he remembered the time she tripped—and the kiss that followed.

She poured coffee for Matt and emptied cookies onto a plate. She watched him eat, enjoying the sight of his strong white teeth crunching the crisp sweet. They didn't speak until he'd eaten two cookies. Jake stopped at one, and eyed Matt as if wondering if he could eat the same amount and then decided not to try.

"I've been thinking. Every boy needs a dog."

She ignored the light that came in Jake's eyes. "Well, just keep thinking it, but don't include us."

"I can take it back if it doesn't work out with you."

"And how do you suppose it could work out?" She glared at him and nodded her head toward Jake who was staring enraptured at his hero. "What about our leaving for the winter? No one's going to rent an apartment to a single mother with a boy and a puppy."

Matt frowned, dark brows winging downward. His eyes were nearly the same color as the coffee in his cup. She looked away before he caught her staring.

"No need to be in any hurry. The snow's not due for a while yet."

Was he procrastinating for them? A good sign.

"Jake, the pup's in the Jeep. I'm sure your mom will let you play with it *temporarily*."

Jake gave a shout and didn't stop to ask permission when he bounded out of the house, slamming the door behind him.

"You undermine my discipline, but then you know that, don't you?"

"Yes, but you don't want to turn into something like your ex, do you?"

"That's certainly food for thought."

"The pup can stay with us until you come back in the spring. Sunny's getting tired of nursing and the pups eat dog food now. I promised them to nearby ranchers but I wanted Jake to have first pick. After that she's going to the vet to be spayed."

She wanted to argue more. It would surely hurt Jake when he had to leave the pup behind and apparently Matt didn't recognize this. On the other hand, there was the promise she'd made to herself to lighten up, that Jake would be okay. The outdoors beckoned to her. "Well, come on then, let's not let Jake have all the fun." She grabbed his hand and pulled him toward the door. "I might as well see the pup too, since you were so generous as to let Jake have the pick of the litter."

His grin was sheepish as he held the door open for her. She brushed close to him deliberately, just to give him pause and didn't miss the intake of his breath. He hid it by running down the steps first, calling back to her, "Last one's a wooden nickel."

"I haven't heard that one in years." She laughed at the two sitting on the ground with the puppy licking first one and then the other.

She sat beside them and immediately the pup changed gears and ran to bounce on her lap. "Hey, take it easy!" She held him down a minute so she could rub his ears gently. The pup wasn't having any of that. He wriggled out of her lap and ran back to Jake and Matt.

"He is a cutie, that's for sure. You ok with leaving him when we move away?"

For a moment, Jake quit petting the dog and then nodded. "It's worth it."

How did he get so sweetly logical in such a short time? It never ceased to amaze her.

"I'm sure you're itching to get back to work. I'll make you a cup of coffee for the road."

He stood up, stretching out his long legs. "I thought maybe you'd like another ride. You seemed to enjoy seeing the deer."

"That might be nice. I'd like to see the deer again." She got the impression he wanted her to go alone. While she would have liked Jake to see the deer too, sometimes a woman had to leave the mother part behind for a time.

"We can drop Jake off at the house and he can play with Sunny."

"That okay with you?" she asked.

Jake nodded.

"Oh, just a minute, you two. I wanted to take some water and a sweater with me this time. I'll be right back." Casey ran back up the steps and into the house where she'd stashed a small backpack.

They drove into the yard. Paco and Matt saddled up the two horses while Jake played with the pups and Sunny. As they headed the horses into the woods, Matt turned back to look at her. Casey thought he was ready to make a smart remark about her speed, but in truth she had encouraged the mare to go a bit faster and the horse was responding.

"You fit here, did you know that?" Matt said. "I didn't expect that." He turned back to look ahead before she could answer.

No matter. She didn't know what to say. She kneed the horse closer. "I challenge you to a race to the meadow," she called out to him.

He turned in the saddle again, a grin curling his lips and his eyes crinkled with unexpressed laughter. "You're joking."

"No, I'm not. I believe me and Sadie here are beginning to be on the same page. We understand each other."

"Sadie?"

"Well, if Jake can name a horse, I might as well do the same. Don't you think the name fits?"

"Immensely," he said, chuckling.

She kicked the sides of the mare and the horse took off at a lumpy gallop, almost catching up with Matthew and Smokey.

"Okay, but it's a ridiculous idea." The wind ate up the rest of his words, as he galloped ahead with the challenge.

Casey waited a second and then turned the mare onto the short cut she'd spied the last time they'd come this way, sure it would take them to the same place. The mare seemed to absorb some of Casey's excitement and loped up and down the little hills of the rougher terrain. It was as if no one had ever asked anything of the mare before, and so she enjoyed the run. Over the last little hill, Casey saw the meadow before her and heard Smokey crashing through the brush behind them. She leaped off the mare and quickly laid out the white tablecloth she'd brought and set down two glass goblets and the bottle of wine Carmen had given her from the house. The hoof beats were almost upon her by the time she finished. She sat and leaned nonchalantly back against a tree trunk, waiting.

When Matt topped the last rise, his look was priceless. His jaw sagged, his eyes widened in surprise.

"What took you guys so long?" Casey asked.

His roar of laughter startled a huge flock of birds in the nearby trees. He slid off his horse and pulled her to her feet, enveloping her in a bear hug. "You are something special, for sure. How did you get the old gal, Sadie is it, to run fast enough to beat us here?"

Casey smiled and hugged him back. "That's our secret. Now sit a spell and have a drink. Then we'll need to head back before they all come looking for us."

When they returned to the house to pick up Jake, Matt took them back to the cabin in the Jeep.

"Can I stay out here and play with the puppy?" Jake asked.

"Sure thing, but don't let him wander too far away," Matt said, as he turned to follow Casey up the steps into the cabin "He might get lost in the woods and brush."

Casey poured them cups of coffee and they sat at the table. "I'm taking Jake in for tests on Monday. We may stay there a few days."

"You mean Center City?"

She nodded. "The Parker Clinic is fine, I love the doctors there. I gave them copies of Jake's records, but I want to confirm Jake's improvements with the Center City doc."

"Want me to drive you there?"

"Do you want to?"

At her unexpected challenge, he got to his feet and walked toward the picture window.

Casey heard the clock ticking in the background as she took in his wide shoulders, tapering down to the narrow waist and—

He whirled to face her. "Casey—damn it, I don't know what to think anymore. Sure, I want to be with you. Then sometimes I don't." He pulled her up by her elbows until she stood facing him.

She felt a lurch of excitement and tried to suppress it. He was so close that she inhaled the man-smell of leather and a slight after-shave that she hadn't detected on him before. He must have used the after-shave for her. He told her once that ranchers never used foo-foos as he called it, because it scared the cattle. Part of her wanted to surrender, to allow herself to melt in his arms, protected by his strength. He would reach out to hold her if she came closer. Buried deep underneath all that guilt he carried, she knew there must be a passionate, loving, and giving man who might never be set free. He might never allow himself to be free. Did she have time to search for the key? Not if he wanted her out by first snow fall. They had to find another place to live and it couldn't be near him. They might have to go to another state, try something new. If she left, it would never be the same between them again.

"You're the most desirable woman I've ever met. I can't seem to get close enough to you."

The underlying sensuality in his voice warmed her, made her want to hear more. His eyes swept over her like a caress, across her face and over her body. He wanted her. That came through loud and clear. She longed for the fulfillment of his lovemaking. Just imagining it brought a flush to her face.

Matt drew her into the circle of his arms and crushed her against him. She felt his warm breath on the top of her head. She let him hold her for a long moment before she stood on tiptoes and pushed him away far enough to hold his face between her hands. Laying her lips against his, she put everything she had into the kiss. He responded with a groan. His probing tongue met hers. The kiss seemed to last a lifetime.

When they came up for air, he rained kisses on her face, touching her gently with his lips. Moving downward, his tongue lingered on the throbbing pulse in her throat.

She never knew which of them came to their senses first. Suddenly there was cold air between their bodies. He looked down at her, eyes filled with regret. "Looks like one of us is always pulling away, doesn't it?"

"I know."

He turned back to look out the window. "The offer still holds. I'll drive you to Center City."

She shook her head, knowing he could see her reflection in the window. "Thanks, but we will manage. I don't know how long we'll be there. You go ahead and do your cowboy stuff."

She knew he wanted to come with them and maybe they would get together, without the problem of a ghost looking over his shoulder. She wasn't ready for a short-term relationship or a long one either. She willed her pulse back to normal, and took a deep breath. He did the same.

"In Arizona, did you take him to the doctors often?" He asked, as if struggling for normalcy.

"We were always at the hospital for one crisis or another."

"Maybe it was too convenient?"

She bristled at the thought of him casting aspersions on her judgment, but held her tongue.

"The folks will be back from their trip to Yellowstone sooner or later," he continued. "I'd like you to meet them."

It didn't mean anything special, she told herself, when his words made her heart flutter. He had made it abundantly clear that he wanted her, desired her, but with no strings attached. She feared she was getting in too deep emotionally to be intimate with him.

They stepped outside. He went down the steps to gather up the pup, who was playing in a pile of dry leaves. "I'll take him home for now, and we'll see about it when you come to visit again."

"Okay, bye puppy." Jake waved at the pup's receding backside as Matt deposited him in the Jeep.

Hanging over the railing of the porch, Casey and Jake watched them leave.

"I liked the pup. Did you?"

"Sure did. Is that really your favorite? He's pretty cute."

"Yeah! I picked him out when we went to the picnic."

"I thought maybe you did, but you know that when we move, you have to leave him here."

Was it time to confide in Jake that they might not be back? No. That would cause him more anxiety than he needed just now. There would be time for the truth later.

During the days that followed, Matt had trouble focusing on his chores. Paco stopped him one morning from feeding the horses a double portion of oats. One day he absentmindedly cut some of Carmela's flowers down when he mowed the yard.

"Hey, Boss, Let me do that. Why don't you take it easy? Maybe you need a vacation, get away for a little bit." Paco told him, a wide grin on his face.

"Nonsense. You're getting as bossy as Carmela." Matt knew he must look like a nut case, since both Carmela and Paco seemed to know how much he missed Casey and Jake.

Nights were the worst, knowing the cabin sat empty. Once he drove over just to sit on the steps. What was getting into him? Why would he want to become involved in anyone's life? Especially since Casey didn't know her own mind or what she wanted out of life. He had no qualms about that. He had everything necessary right here under his boots. He owed a debt to Dorothy's spirit or whatever the hell it was called, and by damn he meant to see it through.

Yet, on another level, he missed the notes in the tumbleweeds. Did she suspect he knew they were hers?

Then, out on a fence check one morning, he found another tumbleweed with a square of paper inside. The odd feeling in the pit of his stomach was hard to ignore as he retrieved the message. What began as a chuckle ended in a roar of laughter as he spread Jake's cartoon figure out on his thigh.

"Great balls of fire!" he crowed, spooking the horse so that he danced sideways.

The realization of what this could mean hit him like a blow to the stomach. It meant she maybe wasn't lonely anymore. She didn't have any sad poems to send out to the world, or it meant she knew Matt had found them.

Which was it? Not knowing made him restless. This is what came of caring about something or someone. It always began to hurt eventually. He knew of only one way to settle it.

The next morning he braked the Jeep in front of Dorothy's house and sat a while staring at it as if he'd never seen it before. Hell, it was just a house, wasn't it? Carmela always believed ghosts lived inside. Casey accused him of *locking* the ghosts inside. If this was what he had done, it was wrong. And it was time to set them free. He lugged in an armload of sacks and boxes, dumping them in the middle of the floor. Then he packed, working up a rhythm while trying not to stop overlong on any one item. He stripped off the bureau tops, unloading clothes from the drawers and stuffing everything in the sacks.

A fine film of dust swirled around him, turbulent, agitated, choking him for a moment. He stopped and cocked his head, listening. He heard an unusual sound, like a long, deep sigh.

"I don't believe in ghosts," he said out loud. Disregarding the dust rising in the air, he continued to pack her possessions away, in a frenzy to finish the job.

Carmela had said she and Paco would take the boxes and sacks to Parker, to the Mission, when he was finished. It was the only way.

When he had it all packed up and stowed in the Jeep, he returned for one last inspection. The dust motes sifted around the living room, touched with sparkle by the morning sun slanting off the patio sliding door. No, he had never believed in ghosts, but he did feel something, someone saying goodbye.

Matt turned away and didn't look back.

CHAPTER 15

In Center City, Casey spent her time calling her editor while she and Jake waited for the appointment with Doctor Watson. The editor remembered her and was glad to hear she had started writing again. When she got off the phone, she took Jake's hands and did a little jig, pulling him in a circle until he started giggling. "They want me to send in some chapters. Isn't that great, son?"

"Sure is. You gonna do that soon as we get back home?"

Back home. No, she wouldn't let negative thoughts dampen her enthusiasm. She was coming to dread seeing those cold white envelopes from the bank with the deposit slip for Richard's check. It was as if he paid them to stay out of his life and the irony was, they were glad to do it. If she could realize her dream and become self-supporting, then Richard's checks for Jake could go toward a college fund and she wouldn't even have to see them every month.

When they entered the clinic for their doctor's appointment, she knew Jake wanted to hold her hand, but his clenched fists held tight to his sides told her he was determined to stand on his own. Matt had a point when he cautioned her to give Jake some space. He made her understand that she was the needy one, and here she always thought it was the other way around.

When they called her name, she and Jake entered the exam room. She was glad to see Dr. Watson's familiar presence. The last time they were at the Parker Clinic, when she'd asked about Dr. Watson, they explained that he often went back and forth between Parker and Center City.

"Mrs. Nichols, so good to see you again.' He turned from looking at some papers and put out his hand. She didn't miss the look of surprise on the doctor's face when he looked at Jake. "Hello there, young man. My, but you've grown in the six weeks since I last saw you."

Jake shook his hand and beamed.

Dr. Watson turned to Casey. "It isn't so much that he's grown, actually, but something I can't put my finger on." He rustled more papers and looked uncomfortable for an instant. "I've arranged for some colleagues to examine your son. They are Colorado resident doctors and can judge his condition with new eyes so to speak."

"But Doctor," she protested. "We especially came here to Center City to see you. I thought it wonderful that you transferred to this hospital from Phoenix. That made my decision to come to Colorado so much easier."

"I appreciate that. I will see to Jacob later. I just wanted the other doctors to check him out first." With that, he nodded and backed out of the door.

Dr. Watson called him Jacob, not the usual Jake. Casey thought his actions were strange and imagined he would return until the nurse came in to tell Jake to take off his shirt and jeans and slide up on the exam table. A phalanx of doctors followed her in.

"Mrs. Nichols," one of them said. "I am Dr. Davidson and this is Dr. Phelps and our resident psychiatrist, Dr. Ruiz. Would you mind waiting outside, please?"

None of the other doctors had ever asked that of Casey, but she complied reluctantly, thinking Colorado might have different methods of dealing with children. Almost thirty minutes dragged by before a nurse asked her to come into the room.

The doctor who spoke to her before said, without preamble, "Your son's doing quite well, Mrs. Nichols. But I don't like the sound of that cough, and you must have noticed his pronounced wheeze."

How could she not notice? He had wheezed off and on for most of his life.

The doctors bent over Jake who was still clad only in his shorts. Casey noticed that his rib cage no longer showed so severely. He was filling out. Was there something they weren't telling her? Why would they need a psychiatrist to examine Jake? Maybe he came along just to observe. There wasn't anything wrong with Jake's mental attitude. He was the most up-beat little kid in the world.

"We'd like to keep him here for observation. Would that be inconvenient?"

Damn their politeness. The Nichols had a hand in this. She could smell it a mile away. They mentioned they had visited the children's ward in Center City. They knew Dr. Watson. Who did they think they were messing with here? Righteous anger sped through her body, giving her adrenaline to face down the wall of implacable eyes looking at her.

"Yes, it would be extremely inconvenient." She struggled to rein in her temper. It wouldn't help matters to come off flaky and out of control. "I don't see any reason to keep him overnight. What did you say your name was?" She asked the doctor who seemed to be in charge.

"Davidson, Dr. George Davidson," he said. "Dr. Watson is relatively new here at our facility and I'm taking over Jacob's case for him."

Had Mrs. Nichols mentioned that name as someone she talked to here? If so, she didn't recall the conversation.

"Ah—we weren't thinking in terms of overnight," another doctor stepped in to say. "We thought perhaps a week of steady quiet under serene conditions might improve his outlook somewhat."

"Jake lives in serene conditions every day of his life now. There is nothing wrong with his outlook. I won't leave him," she said.

"We need to take a series of tests. From what the records reflect, he's getting better, but there's a higher white blood cell count than is normal and we don't know why."

What did that mean, high white cell blood count? Her heart tripped in her chest until she managed to calm herself. That sounded ominous, but her radar was up and she needed another opinion. Her instinct was to bundle Jake up and take him home immediately. Every passing moment warned her that Richard's parents were involved. Richard hadn't wanted his son, but the Nichols were not so likely to give him up. They were so sure they knew what was best for their grandson.

Were they saying she hadn't provided the proper care for Jake? Is that why the psychiatrist was present? Casey glared at her image in the mirror that spanned the wall next to the examination table. Willow thin, white faced, taut like the string on a bow, she might not appear to strangers to be the model of an ideal mother, serene and capable.

Even her hair, the one feature she liked, had betrayed her. The wind had disheveled it, making a golden red encircling her head with curls. For once, she cursed the waywardness of her tresses.

"It's a good idea for your son, Mrs. Nichols. We have a wing made up of boys and girls like Jacob. He could use other children's company."

They must have read in her expression that she remained unconvinced.

"I'm afraid I must insist," the head doctor said sternly, peering at her over his half-frame glasses. "He could have picked up a virus, like valley fever, in layman's terms. We need to check it out."

"No." Casey went cowboy on them with one word, succinct and to the point. "I'll want a second opinion. We go right by the Parker clinic on our way home. They can draw blood and verify your findings and we can go on from there." She walked over to the table where Jake sat up, watching them. She turned to face the doctors and put a hand behind her back to touch him. He laid his on top of hers. She felt his hand spasm. He had been holding on for dear life.

"I suppose that would work. Labs can be wrong, although I have never known ours to be. Do you have a telephone for emergency?" Dr. Davidson asked. Why would he ask a thing like that but for the Nichols' intervention? No, she wasn't paranoid. They wanted a wedge between her and Jake so they could step in. Honestly, if she thought it would be better for him, she might consider it, but he was doing fine.

"We haven't had one all along. Is that so important?"

The Doctor with the glasses pursed his lips. "Yes, at this point in time it could be extremely important. The boy's immune system is trying to tell us something. We want to provide a heart monitor for him to wear for twenty-four hours and you will need to call in both days to assure us it is still in place. It's been my experience that in outlying areas a cell phone isn't reliable."

She found that out already. "That's easy to solve. The Parker Clinic is only sixty miles from our place. He could get the monitor checked out there when the time is up."

Casey waited while the doctors conferred and then Dr. Davidson nodded for the nurse to strap on the monitor for Jake.

"You may take Jacob to the clinic in Parker and have them remove the monitor when the test is finished. By then Dr. Watson will be there again and will see you. That will be satisfactory, on the condition that you call in once a day."

Casey folded her arms across her chest and came to a decision. She knew she wasn't going to win every battle with these doctors and had to concede something. It also didn't make sense that she needed to call just to confirm that he wore the contraption. Since that only made two concessions, she could live with it.

"I have a friend who lives near us. He has a phone and a housekeeper versed in medicine who can help if I need assistance. I want to take my son home." A little mild exaggeration never hurt anything, since Carmela claimed to be a medicine woman.

"Would you mind calling your friend now to make certain it will be possible to use the phone there?"

Good grief, did they think she was such a rotten mother that she would lie about having a friend with a phone? Temper, temper, she cautioned herself. Trying to maintain as much cool control as possible, she walked to the nearest desk where a doctor pointed out a phone she could use. She wondered if the Nichols had promised the hospital a wing or some special operating equipment to gain this much consideration.

"Matt?" After she assured him they were all right, she explained the situation and asked if she could use the phone every day to check with the doctors. "I thought we might stay here a few days but I want to come home today."

"Great. When you get here you can stay at the main house. We have plenty of room and Carmela would be happy."

Casey thought this a good idea. She mentioned that Carmela's name had come up as a person good with medicine and healing. She held her hand over the phone so no one would hear Matt's laugh. He guessed what she must have told them to get Jake back home.

"I'm sure they'd be thrilled to know we have a resident *bruja*. Did you really tell them that?"

"Hmm. No comment."

"I'll get Carmela to make the arrangements. See you both soon."

When she hung up, the head doctor said, "I'd like to speak to you alone, Mrs. Nichols."

"Mom." Jake caught hold of her sleeve. His eyes were shiny with unshed tears.

"Yes, son?" She picked him up off the table and let him stand beside her.

"You're not leaving me here, are you?"

She knelt to face him. "No, Jake. I promise." She took his hand and brought it to her cheek. "Put your clothes on while you're waiting and soon as I get back we'll leave."

"Okay."

"That's my big boy." She stood up. "Wait here, I'll be right back."

Casey followed the doctor into his inner sanctum. He motioned her to a chair and began talking low into his transcriber. She could barely hear but caught the words Jacob and Nichols several times. How rude. He could do this when she wasn't present. She recognized a calculated maneuver to intimidate and she felt proud that it wasn't working.

When she started to get to her feet, he stopped talking into the machine, frowning.

"Ah, Mrs. Nichols." As if he had been unaware that she followed him into the room. He made a few quick notes on a pad, clicked the machine off and looked at her over his half-frame glasses.

He didn't impress her, if that was his intention.

"Jacob is improving in great strides. Just a little more intensive therapy and we'll have him playing outside like a—"

"Like a normal little boy? He *is* a normal little boy—with a problem. He already plays outside. A hospital is not the place for Jake. He needs to be home."

The doctor shook his head, his expression sympathetic "Home?" He raised his eyebrows.

That was when she knew for sure the Nichols had spoken to the doctors here.

"Fresh air and sunlight are placebos. He needs—"

"Fresh air, sunshine, and love. You forgot the love. I love my son and a mother senses when something is wrong and when something is working. There's no need to rush his getting well when he's doing it on his own, slowly but surely."

"Judging from the charts from Phoenix, his change of color, his gaining weight, I'd have to agree that he has indeed made remarkable progress since you brought him to Colorado. We just think we can help him reach optimum health quicker and more efficiently if you left him with us for observation."

"Are these the orders given to you by Colonel and Mrs. Nichols, Jake's father's parents?" It was getting harder and harder for her to refer to them as simply grandparents. They were becoming *the enemy*.

The doctor ruffled through papers on his desk, his poise momentarily disappearing. He cleared his throat. "Certainly his grandparents would have their only grandson's best interest at heart and they can well afford any treatment we have to offer."

He obviously meant that she probably couldn't afford the best for him. "This is about money, isn't it? You aren't worried about my son's well-being. If you were, you would have to concede that he is improving beyond anyone's expectations. Did the Nichols offer you an endowment?"

Casey glared at the doctor with narrowed eyes, thinking how selfish people were when it came to money and how having so much of it caused such arrogance. How could the Nichols presume to know what was best for Jake when their own son didn't care? Her rejection of Richard was the same as rejecting them and they couldn't let it be.

She rose out of the chair and leaned forward over the desk. She hit her fist on the center of his piled papers, sending them scattering. "I don't care about their money. I don't care about their influence. I am taking my son home. They must have told you I received full, uncontested custody of him and by law, neither you nor anyone else can forcibly keep him from me."

Her confidence increased when her voice didn't waver. Months ago she would never have had the guts to confront this authority figure and talk to him this way. How did Matt say it? Mama Quail, defending her own. She had a completely new attitude and that pleased her immensely.

He leaned back and sighed, pushing away papers that he had obviously readied for her to sign. "See the nurse for check-out papers. I'll authorize his release, but you will have to sign that you accept the responsibility of his release without our approval. Furthermore, it probably won't be necessary for you to stop at Parker to get more blood work done. We might have been a little hasty about that, upon looking over the records again."

"Of course I'll sign papers accepting responsibility for taking Jake home." The Nichols had been so certain she would crumble and leave Jake that they had already made up papers to that effect. She turned toward the door and shut it firmly behind her.

When she went into the room to collect Jake, the absolute surprise and joy on his face nearly did her in. The monitor bulged through his Tee shirt and he looked ready to burst with importance as if he wore a badge. The nurse gave her written instructions.

"Come on, son. Let's go. Maybe we can locate a root beer float somewhere."

"Whew! I thought I was a goner," he said, his eyes serious.

Another thing he learned from Matt. She grinned at him. "Nope. I said I promised, didn't I?" It was then she realized that he kept all his fears inside. He probably had feared his father would take him in the divorce and later that his grandparents would take him. It might hurt him even more to know that his father hadn't wanted him, but he would never find that out from her.

Out on the street, the wind buffeted her calf-length denim skirt against her legs, tangling the material with her boots so that she had a hard time walking. She would be glad to get out of the city, to climb into her jeans and sweat shirt.

Jake took her hand, wanting to play the part of her protector when they crossed the busy street. There was so much traffic due to the city being abuzz with the annual balloon flights, which would last the week according to Matthew. It would have been something to take Jake to, but the wrong time for both of them. Casey pulled up at a fast food drive-thru to get Jake's root beer float and then edged the car out of town, heading up toward the foothills. In a few hours, they would be home.

Home. A word the doctors had used disparagingly. Home is where we are together, she decided. They were family, just the two of them. That part was okay, but she knew they couldn't stay in the little rustic cabin, hidden away forever. Matt had pointed out all the dangers of winter and she had listened without wanting to. Eventually they would have to come out into the real world. Although there was nothing wrong with her home schooling, Jake should be around other kids.

On the way to the ranch they talked. More and more, he was opening up to her. She wished it would come as easy for her to learn to trust again as it seemed to be for Jake.

"Thanks for not leaving me there, Mom."

Did he know she stood silently at his opened bedroom door sometimes during the night, listening for labored breathing and to check on him? She hoped not. And if he did, he never let on. "It's okay, kiddo. We can do what the doctors want us to do and still stay home. That works out good, don't you think?"

He made a high-five sign, knowing she didn't want to do it while driving.

"You didn't put any poems in the tumbleweeds in a long time. Did you forget?"

Visions of the tumbleweeds brought up a picture of Matt. It was at once comforting to think of his strength, his stalwart loyalty, and his exciting, rugged profile. Still, she also had to temper those thoughts with his stubborn resistance to change.

"Are we going to keep staying in the little house? You like Matt, don't you? I sure do."

"He's a good friend, even if we haven't known him long. Carmela says time isn't important when it comes to knowing someone."

She reached over and ruffled his hair. "You're right. About the tumblewords. When we get back, we'll send off some more messages."

They passed by the main house on their way to the cabin but no one was outside. Once inside her cozy little home, she poured a cup of coffee from the thermos that sat filled on the counter. She forgot to take it to Center City. The coffee was cold but she needed the caffeine-hit right away.

"Get some stuff packed," she said. "Just enough to tide us over so we don't have to bop back here every day."

"Wow! Are we really going to stay at Matt's? I thought you just told the doctors that to get away."

She pointed to the monitor he wore. "No. While you're wearing that gizmo we have to call in both days."

Jake gave his impression of an Indian war whoop and ran back into his room. She smiled, wondering how that would affect his monitor. She heard dresser drawers open, and the closet door slam shut two or three times. Likely as not he was packing his toys and Game Boy while his clothes lay untouched in the dresser.

Casey sighed, wondering what the next few days would hold.

CHAPTER 16

When the car crunched up the gravel drive, Jake wriggled with excitement, even though the seat belt hampered him from jumping up and down.

"Hey, cool it! We don't know what all that jumping around is doing to your monitor." With so many misgivings, she nearly turned the car around after they parked in the circular driveway. Did she want to get this close to Matt for even such a short period? Part of her gloried in the idea of seeing him every day in ordinary circumstances and part of her feared that if he pressed her, she wouldn't always be able to back away.

Jake refused to be still. Casey gritted her teeth. Not often did she lose patience, but her mind was going in six directions at once. "What did I tell you, young man? Calm down. If you weird up your monitor they might come up here to get you."

"Hi, pard. Hello, Casey. Here, let me get those." Matt stepped off the porch and reached for the suitcases.

Jake held onto a box. "I can carry my own stuff," he proclaimed.

"And that's a fact. Bring your stuff then and Paco will get the rest." Matt touched Casey's arm. "I see you brought your laptop. Good. Keep you busy."

"I left it behind once before when I went on a trip." She smoothed her hair and laughed at the remembrance. "I developed withdrawal symptoms and had to find a computer store just to go inside and smell them."

He laughed.

Carmela bustled down the front steps, followed by Paco, who had been stacking wood near the fireplace. Carmela kissed the top of Jake's head. He set down his box so he could shake Paco's hand.

"Oh, we will have such a grand time," the housekeeper said, hugging Jake now that he was unprotected by the box he'd been holding in front of his chest.

He giggled and looked up at Casey as if he needed rescuing from being smothered in Carmela's ample bosom.

"Enough of that hugging stuff," Matt said. "Let's get them moved into their rooms and then I'll let Jake help me. I'm horse-shoeing today."

"Wow!" Jake followed close behind as Matt led the way.

"You got a choice. This was Mom and Pop's room. Twin beds, you can bunk here together, or if Jake's brave and wants to stay alone, he can use my old room. I outgrew it, but the folks kept my things in it."

Casey knew the answer. Everyone watching Jake knew it as he gazed up at his idol, eyes filled to the brim with happiness. He had never slept that far from her except when he stayed in the hospital. He climbed up the winding staircase to the attic room, only looking back once. Matt regarded her, his eyes unreadable under the fringe of dark lashes. He waited and she knew he thought Jake needed space on his own, separation from her constant presence.

She agreed with him.

"Hey, Mom," he called from inside the room. "Neat! Even my own window." He came out of the doorway and looked down at Matt. "I promise not to get into your things," he said, eyes serious.

"Heck, nothing to get into up there. Help yourself,"

After they ate a lunch of huge beef sandwiches on the wide veranda overlooking the sloping grasslands, Jake yawned.

"Hey kiddo. Time you caught a few Zs."

For once, he didn't argue with her. Carmela led him away while he chattered to her, telling about the special toys and computer game he kept in the box.

When they were alone, Matthew reached across the space between the rockers to take her hand. "You're beat, aren't you?"

"No, I'm okay. It's good of you to let us intrude like this. Otherwise, without a phone handy, I'm sure they'd have tried to insist Jake stay there." She felt revived—and lighter, as if a weight had toppled off her shoulders. It felt good to be surrounded by people who cared and would help her if she needed it. She knew she was strong, but she also had to admit that having someone share the load was good too, if only for a little while.

"Want to take a walk? I'd like to hear what the doctors had to say." There was a hint of amusement in his eyes when she hesitated. "Afraid of me?" he challenged.

She smiled at the cocky tilt of his head. Afraid wasn't the word. Her most pressing thought was the need to put her hands in the hair at the back of his neck and pull him close for a kiss. Afraid? She'd show him.

"Walking sounds good. I need to clear my head."

He put his hand on her shoulder. His fingers seemed to burn through her clothing into her skin. He was so much taller than she was and she always got a lump in her throat when he tilted his head a bit to the side and leaned toward her, his mouth ready to plunder hers.

"Take your sweater, the air's a little nippy."

In spite of the mid-afternoon sun and cloudless sky, the air was tingly cool and crisp. Did that portend the beginning of fall? Every time she thought of fall and winter it was like a huge, gloomy cloud spread over her the gloom, enveloping her in a prison she couldn't seem to escape. She could move to Parker, Center City or go on to New Mexico. She had a girl friend from college that she had corresponded with while living in Phoenix who had invited her to Albuquerque. But those weren't options she wanted to take and she knew it.

Matt grabbed the throw that lay over the porch railing. "We might want to sit and rest. The view from the top of the mesa is a breath-taker, I warn you."

As they stepped down off the back porch, he took her arm to steer her over the uneven ground until they hit the flat meadowland. "We don't get much of a fall, usually. Sometimes we go from summer to winter, boom, just like that."

"Oh."

"Thinking about what I told you? That you couldn't stay in the cabin?"

"Yes. I don't want to go back to Phoenix. Maybe we could settle in Center City."

What did she want him to say? It wasn't clear even to her, but he must know when she left, things would be different between them. Maybe that was it—there wasn't that much between them. Yet. Still, she knew better.

"What about Parker? Is the town too small for you? My folks would be there if you need them."

"Jake and I, we do okay on our own. But thanks for the idea. Parker's nice. We'll see."

She didn't think it would be wise to be so close to him, available to visit conveniently when he wanted to. Could she keep turning down his advances if he continued to make them?

Matt stopped at the edge of the clearing and they stood close to each other, looking back toward the house, which they could no longer see. He reached to touch her hair.

"Your hair amazes me. I can't get used to it. It's like a sun-storm."

She smiled up at him, enjoying the compliment. "That's an odd way of putting it, but thank you. I've given up on trying to control it and mostly let it do its own thing. My father had hair as straight and dark as yours, but mother's genes stuck me with this kinky-curly mane. She warned me when I was a kid that I might as well give up trying to tame it."

"Does she have long hair like yours?"

Casey didn't know how to answer that. She hadn't spoken of her parents in a long time. Richard never seemed interested and she was still in the process of forgiving them for leaving her. Even though now she realized that her mother couldn't help dying and her father probably knew it was better to leave his young daughter with his sister than struggle with trying to cope with his life. That was one reason she'd bonded so tightly with Carmela. Her aunt hadn't wanted her either.

"I don't have parents. My mother died when I was very young and my father couldn't take it. He left me with my aunt." Before he could say anything, she moved away from the personal feelings and changed the subject. "A lot of women wear short curly hair. Sometimes I think I'd like to try that."

"No!" His voice rang out in the quiet meadow and then he looked sheepish, ashamed of his outburst. "I mean, it's your hair, but..."

"Don't worry, it won't happen anytime soon." It pleased her to think he cared about her hair. She knew that wasn't all he liked by the way his eyes devoured her. The tension crackled between them as she returned his bold look.

They moved out of sight of the buildings, walked a while longer, and climbed a slight incline until they reached the edge of a canyon. Below lay a green valley surrounded by walls of rock and earth.

She sucked in a deep breath. "Oh my, this is amazing. I've never seen anything as beautiful."

"Told you so." Matt's voice was filled with pride. "Want to sit here and watch the wind blow over the mesa? I don't imagine there are any bugs crawling around on the ground."

Casey smiled. "Bugs and I have an understanding. I leave them alone and they usually ignore me. Besides that, any mother with a six-year-old boy can take whatever the bugs of the world can dish out."

She glanced at Matt and caught a sharp look of pain in his eyes before he hid it. Had her words made him think of what might have been if his son had lived? No, it must have been only her imagination because he laughed at her words as he spread out the blanket.

She like the sound of his laughter. It emanated from deep inside his chest. And his teeth flashed white against the mahogany of his tanned skin when he smiled. And his lips...

There she went again, fantasizing about his mouth, as if she could feel it warm and yielding against her own.

In one accord, they removed their boots and socks, wriggling their feet in the cold air. They sat close, not touching until he took hold of her shoulders, turned her around toward him, and brought his mouth down on hers in a searing kiss that nearly melted her toenails.

"Open your mouth," he whispered hoarsely, his warm breath tantalizing her lips.

She caught a glimpse of the naked hunger and need burning in his eyes. The sun's rays left her face as his head blocked it out, blocked out everything but the fiery need that pulsed through her body. She smelled his man-scent, a mixture of leather and horse.

Crushing her against him, he fired hot kisses down her neck, causing a flood of heat to swamp her entire body. Yet, his passion was touchingly restrained. He groaned and made as if to roll away.

"Don't. Don't stop." She grabbed at his shirtsleeve and pulled him back.

"Casey, sweetheart," he murmured, smashing the material between them. He slowly unbuttoned her shirt, and hesitating only a moment, she undid the snaps on his. She reached her arms around him, snuggling up to his bare chest a moment, feeling the pounding of his heart against her cheek.

He slipped the shirt off her shoulders. His kisses moved from the nape of her neck down to the end of one shoulder. Then he touched his mouth to her hardened nipples. He caressed each breast with his lips. His callused fingers rippled across her stomach, shooting wonderful chills up and down her body. He stopped a moment and with one last questioning look into her eyes, he unzipped the fly of her jeans and sat up to pull them off her legs. While he divested himself of his Levi's, she slipped out of the last of her clothing. She closed her eyes, waiting.

He lay next to her and in a second had flipped off the shirt she had covered herself with.

"So beautiful. I never imagined..."

The pungent smell of pine needles crushed beneath them wafted up into the air. He leaned on his elbow, his eyes filled with desire, his voice husky. "Casey, I don't want you to be sorry. I need you so much. I've never felt this way before. I'm on fire. Help me, girl, help me," he groaned as she pulled him to her, holding his face between her hands, raining kisses over his closed eyelids, his nose, his mouth.

They moved closer together, her body tuned to his, feeling each other's heartbeats. She reached down and caressed him, his hardness rousing her to heights she had never even imagined. He hesitated briefly at her bold touch, and then slowly, tantalizingly, his hand moved between her legs to caress her. He bent to kiss her breasts then moved on to her flat stomach, his hot tongue teasing against her cool nakedness. She gasped when his kisses continued down her thigh and into her innermost place, now throbbing uncontrollably. Trembling on the edge of a precipice, she put her hands on each side of his head and pulled him gently upward.

When he entered her, her body was warm, moist and ready. They moved together, at first gently, and when he cried out, their bodies merged as if one. She lost the last bit of restraint and abandoned herself to the unexpected rapture overtaking her senses, blocking out time and space—everything but that moment of ecstasy when she felt as if she'd left her body behind and soared. She knew he felt it too by the sudden tensing of his body and the groan that escaped him. Words of love flew from her lips without thought. She heard the sharp intake of his breath, and then he kissed her tenderly, his lips moving over her face, nuzzling into her hair.

Did he realize she had never experienced this intensity of pleasure before? Never had such total abandonment come to her, in all her years of marriage. She hated to open her eyes. When she floated back to earth, she felt inexplicably shy, and tried to cover her nakedness by reaching for his shirt, but he wouldn't allow it. He brushed away her flustered attempts with gentle hands. She felt the hardness, the calluses on his palms when he lovingly ran them over her body as if needing to memorize it.

His touch stirred tendrils of desire not yet used up. The soft mountain breeze floated gently over their damp, naked bodies, bringing exquisite little rippling sensations of cold. He hadn't spoken one word of love during their lovemaking, and she remembered, flushing, that she had blurted out her love for him. She lay back to watch the cloud-streaked sky as the sun shot shafts of color over the fading afternoon. Tears trickled down her cheeks. He kissed the corners of her eyes and wiped away the trail of tears with his thumbs.

"*Querido, yo te amo*. That was so—"

She understood his meaning, which made it even worse. She had to stop him from saying words he had to say in Spanish because he couldn't speak them in English. She leaned over and touched her lips to his, savoring the feel of his skin against hers. He might begin to worry about commitment, since he was an old-fashioned man.

"I love you," were the only words she wanted to hear and she bit her bottom lip in an effort not to say again the words he would not say.

"Don't spoil it with talk," she whispered.

He raised her hands to his lips and kissed them, his lips pausing on each finger separately, as if he couldn't stop touching her. When he released her and lay back, looking up at the tree spread out over them, she too lay back and, with eyes closed, made a vow that she would fight against time to release him from the shell he had wrapped around himself. Beneath the rough, hardened exterior he had developed over the years as a barrier to pain was the vulnerable, loving person she felt sure he could be. Would she have the time and energy to scrape away the granite until that fragile center of his soul lay exposed to her? Exposed so she could nurture it back to health.

Time—she would need plenty of it. And she wasn't sure she had the luxury of time.

She snuggled close to him, pulling the covers over them to shelter their bodies as they dozed.

CHAPTER 17

It had been only yesterday afternoon since they had made love. Although Casey saw the banked fires deep within Matt's dark eyes, he maintained a cool aloofness, as if he might already regret his loss of control. They were sitting on the front porch, she in the swing, he on the steps, leaning against the railing.

"Jake likes Paco a lot. You jealous?" she teased.

He grinned. "Like you used to be with me?"

So, he knew she had been a little envious of the quick masculine bonding he'd developed with Jake. She made a wry face. "You're right, I was jealous. But only because Jake had always been content just to be with me."

"He's still content with you, but you have to give him room to expand and grow."

"My baby. However, yes, I know that now. It's one of the things I've learned since coming out here." She decided not to push. She knew he was capable of deep feelings and she would never settle for anything less than his complete love. His lovemaking told her he had a romantic soul. She only had to find the key.

He broke the silence between them. "You did the right thing, bringing Jake here. I've seen a difference in him—an amazing difference. He's a happier, healthier kid now."

Casey knew the truth of Matt's words and they warmed her heart.

The sun sifted down through the old cottonwood tree in the front yard, working its way across the taut planes of his high cheekbones, moving along the ridge of his jutting, masculine nose. She felt a stab of envy that it wasn't her touching him.

"I'm not doing a roundup this fall, like usual."

"Oh?"

"No. Pop won't be back to help in time, and he likes to get in on it. The cattle aren't scattered either, they're mostly staying close. Just over the ridge to the north, there's a rim rock canyon that keeps them from spreading out too far."

He looked at her, his expression serious. "That's why I think this is going to be a damned hard winter. When the cattle didn't move out like usual, I noticed some are already growing in patches of heavy winter coats. It won't be long before the first snow."

Casey felt a thrill of elation at the huskiness of his voice in spite of words she didn't want to hear. "Please," she said, "Let's not speak of our moving, at least for the time being. It involves a lot more than you'd imagine."

"I'm not talking about the city. You could move the sixty miles into Parker for the winter. It's a good little town. The folks like it. You'd have someone there to help you if you needed it. The clinic, too."

It was a good sign that he wanted his parents to keep an eye on them. But it had to be her choice and she didn't need anyone watching over them. She could continue to home school Jake but didn't he need to be with other kids his age? They studied during the day and sometimes in the evening, which were more concentrated hours than he would have had to do at school. It seemed to be paying off, with his developing a hunger to learn and a strong curiosity about the world in general.

"Look, I know we can't live out here forever. But right now, it's what both Jake and I need. Can you just let it be for now? I'll know when it's time, I promise."

He shrugged.

She liked the way the material of his shirt moved sinuously across the wide expanse of his shoulders. The white tee shirt he wore underneath accentuated the butternut color of his skin.

She closed her eyes for a moment to savor the thought—to remember the feel of his skin beneath her palms. There wasn't an inch of him she hadn't explored and it was the same with him, yet they were sitting like two polite strangers.

Was he so insensitive that he didn't feel, then or now, her need for him—a need that went beyond the physical?

Perhaps he did and it scared the hell out of him. That would be natural, since he clung to the past as if it were a lifeboat in a river of rapids.

"I guess it could get lonesome out here in the winter for a woman alone," he persisted, more than likely to break the silence.

"Carmela stays here. And your mother lived through it for at least thirty years." *Not to mention Dorothy.*

"They weren't alone."

Neither am I. You just don't know it yet, Mister Matthew Tyree.

"You can get out, go to Parker or Center city even in the dead of winter, can't you?" she asked.

"Parker's okay, but I never liked the city. I suppose you do, coming from Phoenix. Symphonies, ballet, plays, movies, museums, libraries, that sort of thing?"

"I thought I'd miss them. They were always there, available, and I took them for granted. Phoenix is a relatively large city. At one time I would have imagined it lonely anywhere else."

"Has it changed?"

"Yes. Being here with Jake has made me realize that loneliness..." She paused, not sure how to continue.

He waited in patient silence. As if he really wanted to hear what she had to say.

"Loneliness doesn't come from outside a person, it comes from inside. Feelings of not belonging, of separation, of abandonment come from yourself, not from others. It took all these years to learn that. You've known it forever, haven't you?"

He smiled, a thoughtful smile that just curved his lips. "I've never thought of it as anything you could put a name to like loneliness. Dorothy and I grew up together. We married out of high school and it wasn't something I studied about, being lonely, until..." He raised his hands and let them fall back on his thighs.

Was it possible to separate this man from his past and bring him into the present? Was he worth the trouble to try?

"Matt." Casey spoke softly, striving for the right words. "When I first came here, all I thought about was Richard. How much I hated him for the way he treated Jake and how he was with me. Thoughts of him consumed me. This meant he still had power over me. I remembered how, over the years he made me so insecure and dependent upon him for everything. He took control by making me powerless. I finally came to one conclusion."

"What was that?" he asked when she hesitated.

She still didn't answer right away and the silence strung out between them. Finally, she said, "I realized that we are born alone and we die alone. In between we just 'borrow' the people who touch our lives in both good and bad ways." She took a deep breath and continued before she lost her courage. "You mourn for Dorothy, who died eight years ago, because you blame yourself-for driving—for being alive—I don't know. I hated Richard because I thought I must be to blame for our failed marriage. Both of us are wrong to continue to hold on to the past, to the guilt, to blame ourselves."

There, she'd said it. She listened to the crickets in the nearby brush. Birds chirped in the branches of the oak tree.

"I know." His words hung on the air.

What did he say? Had her imagination taken over her hearing?

He frowned and shifted his weight on the steps. He was only sitting there to distance himself, instead of sitting next to her on the swing. She took this as a promising sign, that he hadn't gained complete control of his emotions, that his grip was not as iron-strong as he pretended.

He stretched out his long legs and leaned back against the porch railing. "Right now I'm having trouble seeing her face. It's all getting blurry," he admitted reluctantly. "But I don't want that to happen. She's all I ever had."

"You always had yourself in there somewhere," Casey said.

"Maybe. But that was never important." His lips straightened in a stubborn line.

She got up from the swing and sat down next to him on the porch steps while he moved his legs to accommodate hers on the lower one.

"Are you sorry we made love?" Her voice went up a notch on the end and she cleared her throat.

The hard set to his jaw, the muscles working, the jutting of his chin, warned her she might have gone too far too fast.

"Oh, God, no!" He turned to stare into her face, his eyes devouring her features as if he wanted never to forget her. He engulfed her hand in his. The warmth and hardness of his palms sent a current of electricity down her spine and across the back of her neck. He brought her hands to his lips. "No, I wouldn't regret that—ever."

It was coming together. It had to come together. He had to let go of the past eventually. She just needed patience and that was one of her virtues.

Only, would she have the time? With winter coming on, she agreed with him that they couldn't stay in the cabin. If she left now, even for a town sixty miles away, that was like a couple of hundred miles in the dead of a Colorado winter. He would close up on her again and she would have to start all over. Or maybe they would both have time to reconsider and the magic would be gone.

How did she proceed slowly—with haste?

CHAPTER 18

Matt went out to work early each morning and came home late for the next few days. He gave her only brief nods when they met and the silence between them felt like stilettoes in her heart. Why had she let herself fall before he did?

Several evenings they all ate together and Jake chattered on, oblivious to any strain between the adults. Casey looked across the table at Matt, his hair still wet from his shower. It was hard to maintain an even conversation. When she heard the shower running in the evening after he came home, she could imagine his gorgeous body standing in the hot stream of water. She wanted to be in there with him. She fantasized how it would be to rub soap all over him and feel the muscles and sinew beneath the silky water. But it wasn't only the passion she wanted to awaken in Matt. That was already there. It was his heart she needed to open. The hold on his past that kept him detached had to be exorcised. But he had to do it.

At night, she lay awake, hearing him pass by her room to go to his. Once he stopped in the hallway in front of her door. Her heartbeat thudded in her ears. *Turn the knob. Come to me.* She rolled over and rubbed the frustrated tears from her eyes as his footsteps receded down the hallway to his room. It had become torment to be so near to him and yet so far. Did he feel anything? Could he feel the pain that had to be shooting out of her very skin? It was hard to tell from looking into those dark, unfathomable eyes.

One morning when she entered the kitchen, Carmela was making breakfast, as usual. "Want some pancakes? You're too skinny. You would not make a shadow, standing sideways." They both laughed at her ongoing joke.

"Matt out working already?" Casey asked.

Carmela smiled, but her eyes looked sad. "He is away very much lately. I did not know it takes so much time to mend a few fences."

"Doesn't Paco go with him?"

"No, he does not wish anyone with him. That is why I know he is not just mending fences. He is thinking. Matthew is like his father. They like to be alone when they are thinking."

"What do you suppose he is thinking about so much?" Casey prompted.

Carmela flapped her large white apron toward Casey. "You know, *mihija*. You know what is troubling him. He wants to give up the past and yet he fights against it. He is a smart man. He knows he cannot hold on to the past and the future at the same time." She pulled up a chair and sat facing Casey.

Blue eyes looked into intense dark eyes for a long moment and then Casey sighed. "Maybe he knows that deep inside, but it might all sink in too late. I have a feeling when we leave here, we won't be back."

"Patience, little one, have patience. I have been known to predict the future. But I will not say what I think. That would be too easy. You both need to work it out between you so that it will always be settled, never to come up again."

Casey reached for Carmela's hand. "You're so wise. The Tyrees are lucky to have had you and Paco as a part of their family all these years."

Carmela got to her feet and went back to stir a pot on the stove. The marvelous smells wafted up, thick enough to see almost. "We are all lucky. Did I tell you Matt has planned a grand barbecue tomorrow?"

"Of course you didn't. You were going to keep it a secret until you couldn't hold it any longer," Casey said. "Jake will love that idea. He has to go back to the clinic next week and then we can return to our cabin."

"There is another surprise," Carmela said smugly. "Mr. Tyree and Theresa will be here. They called Matthew and are in Parker now."

"I'll be so glad to meet them. Guess I'll sit out here and wait for Jake to wake up." Since Carmela wanted to continue her cooking, Casey took her cup of coffee out on the porch.

When Jake came down, she asked the usual mother questions about brushing his teeth. She didn't have to ask about combing his hair. Since Matthew had shown him how he combed it down and then slicked over it with a comb full of water, Jake had neat hair. Perversely, she missed the haystack look he'd had before in the mornings.

"Jake, this is going to be an exciting time for you. We can go to Parker to take off your monitor tomorrow maybe, and..." She looked at him mischievously, enjoying the inquiring look he shot her.

"Matt is having another barbecue and Mr. and Mrs. Tyree are coming."

"Wow!" He jumped up and down, spilling the orange juice Carmela had poured for him.

Casey thought that monitor was in for a lot of questions, but maybe they took into consideration the age of the patient. She didn't say anything to Jake, not wanting to damper his excitement. It was time to take the gizmo off anyway.

The next morning excitement filled the air and surrounded the ranch house. Jake bounded out of bed at dawn, waiting. Paco had set up tables in the front yard under the trees. Carmela let Casey have the run of her kitchen so she made two cherry pies, Jake's favorite, a lemon meringue and an apple pie, which she would serve hot with slices of cheese.

She didn't see Matt anywhere around. He was probably doing some last minute mending of fences in case his dad inspected, Casey imagined.

A large, shiny pickup crunched up the trail and slipped through the gate before any of them noticed. It was the Tyrees, and Matt's father laid on the horn, as if they might not notice his entrance. She had trouble picturing Matt doing something like that.

Carmela and Paco ran forward, while Casey and Jake hung back until the couples embraced and said their hellos.

Mr. Tyree was almost as tall as Matt, heavier, but still in good shape for his age. Shuffleboard must agree with him, Casey thought. Mrs. Tyree was short and slender, her hair iron gray and pulled back with a turquoise and silver barrette at the back of her neck. They both wore western attire, with a lot of turquoise and silver. They looked tan, fit, and happy.

"So this is Casey and little Jake." Mrs. Tyree approached Casey, shook hands, and knelt in front of Jake. "You don't mind if I give you a big grandma hug, do you?"

"I reckon not," Jake said, drawing the words out.

They all laughed. "I can tell Matthew has been an influence here," Mrs. Tyree said when they recovered.

Just then, Matt made his appearance from the house. Apparently, he had slipped in the back door and washed up. He had slicked his hair down with water, and he wore a clean shirt, with his white tee shirt peeking out the opened neck, and the usual jeans and boots. He put his hat on Jake's head. "Where's your hat, big feller?"

Jake looked up at his idol and swallowed, as if he might be chastised for a mistake. "It's at the cabin. I left it there and Mom won't let us go get anything."

"Okay, blame it on poor ole mom," Casey said. She looked up at the people around her. "I didn't want him to get the rest of his games from there, is all," she said. "I'm trying to wean him away from them. There's so much outdoors for him to investigate."

"Right you are!" Mr. Tyree's voice boomed out. "No need to sit and play games when there's work to be done. Matt, did you show him how to brand cattle yet or help you mend fences?"

Matt grinned. "Not likely. Casey keeps a tight rope on him. I don't think she'd go for that."

She glared at Matt and threw the ball back in his court. "They're teasing, Jake. Don't look at me like that. I haven't said you couldn't do any of those things if *anyone* had asked you to."

"Touché," Mrs. Tyree said, laughing. "I think you're bested in this conversation, my dear."

He grinned. "So what's unusual about that? You do it all the time."

Smells coming from the house and Paco's barbecuing were beginning to make Casey's stomach growl. The cool, nippy air smelled fresh and brought with it a chill off the snow-covered mountains. While everyone visited, Casey stood on a chair and looked over the trees tops toward the ridge of mountains. When had the snow line become so low? That had to be a signal winter was on its way. She tried to not let that put a damper on the day.

By the time Paco had the huge piece of beef on the table, which he sliced and pulled apart, the three women brought out prodigious trays of food. They loaded the table with fresh and tender corn on the cob, grown in the back by the bunkhouse, along with sliced tomatoes, grown by Carmela near the mint bed. Pitchers of lemonade and iced tea, mint and lemon to flavor, and homemade rolls. Mrs. Tyree had brought a huge pot of baked beans, and there was the potato salad of Carmela's, Casey wished she had brought her camera. She'd probably never again see such amazing food. Yet, a camera wouldn't have done justice to the delightful smells.

"Call me Theresa," Mrs. Tyree said to Casey when they sat down to eat.

How great that sounded! Casey felt right at home, part of the family. "Thank you, Theresa. I've certainly enjoyed staying here, although Matt hasn't allowed me to help in any way."

"Carmela and Paco, you've outdone yourselves as usual," Mr. Tyree said. "If we could take you along with us to some of our potlucks, we'd be the toast of the whole blamed state," he told them.

Casey enjoyed the way Carmela and Paco lightened with the praise and soaked up the compliments. Probably Matt appreciated them in his own way, but he seemed to take them for granted and didn't appear to be that forthcoming with praise. At least she hadn't heard it from him. But maybe it wasn't that way at all, since both Carmela and Paco doted on Matt as if he belonged to them.

Matt was very attentive to both her and Jake. He looked handsome in his red plaid flannel shirt and denim vest. He wore his Stetson when he wasn't sitting talking to them, and she loved the endearing hat-line around his head, that she longed to smooth away.

"Jake, I believe you've just about eaten enough. Don't you want to save room for pie?" She looked at the sauce on his chin and refrained from wiping it with her napkin.

"Good gravy! Carmela said you'd baked a lot of pies." Theresa said. "Our whole family has always been pie-crazy but none of us women-folk ever made time to bake pies and it's a darn sure thing the men wouldn't do it."

Matt looked at Jake and then at Casey. A mischievous look came over his face. "Casey's afraid Jake will get so big he won't fit through the cabin doors. You did good, son, but your mom's probably right. Save room for the pie."

After they finished and compliments flew around the table about Casey's pies, the women cleared the table and Matthew helped bring in the platters of leftover meat. As soon as he went outside to join the men, Casey knew she was in for the third degree from his mother.

"Sit, sweetie. Carmela will wash and I'll dry later. No room for three butts in this kitchen."

There was plenty of room, but Casey sat at the table, waiting.

"So. How did things work out for you two while Carmela and Paco were gone? You said he wouldn't let you help, or at least cook a few meals? Not even bake pies or cookies?"

Casey shook her head. "Nope. He refused to have anyone cook for him. Said it did him good to lose a pound or two without Carmela's wonderful food."

Carmela beamed and continued to wash dishes. Theresa sat down across from Casey. The older woman's eyes were mirrors of Matt's. Her son took after his father in size, but the dark thick lashes and the deep coffee colored eyes were the same as his mother's.

"I can't help but see something between you two. A mother knows. I don't want to pry, dear, but if there *is* something going on, it would be an answer to my prayers. We miss the ranch terribly, but neither of us can stand being around our son when he insists on wearing sackcloth and flagellating himself. My God, it's been eight years, hasn't it, Carmela?" She didn't wait for an answer.

Casey wondered how both women got a word in edgewise, since they each loved to talk so much. What could she say about her and Matt? She didn't want his mother to guess that they'd made love. That was a secret she knew

Matt wouldn't want to share either. Pride prevented her from laying her heart on the line to Theresa. If Matt couldn't say the word "love," she didn't want anyone knowing how badly it hurt.

She reached across the table to lay her palm over Theresa's folded hands. "I do care for Matt. He and Jake are like they've always known each other. I am amazed at that. But—"At the older woman's raised eyebrow, so like Matthew's expression, she drew in a deep sigh and continued. "He's like a wounded eagle, one of those birds he showed us over at...Dorothy's place."

Theresa's eyes widened. "He took you there?"

"Yes, he did. And to tell the truth—" She looked up at Carmela who stood by, enraptured by the conversation. "I did sense someone's spirit there, but it also seemed like a sad spirit, if there is any other kind. Like a lost soul left behind who wanted to move on."

"Yes!" Theresa clasped Casey's hand in hers with a slight tremble. "That's what Carmela has been saying all along and I've agreed. Dorothy is trapped inside that house and inside my son and it's not her wish, I know it isn't."

The conversation was growing somewhat weird with Carmela crossing herself and Mrs. Tyree so excited. Casey had to back off a little and gain some space. "Anyway, I don't have the time or energy to fix him. Even if I could."

"Baloney. I see love in your eyes and I see it deep in his. You just have to make time for it to come out."

"That's a luxury we apparently don't have. Matt wants us to be out of the cabin before the first snowfall. He says it's for our own good and I'm sure he's right. But I've the feeling that we can't start all over again where we left off if Jake and I leave."

Mrs. Tyree looked thoughtful and Carmela went back to working in the kitchen.

Before they had a chance to say anything else, they heard Jake shout. Casey leaped to her feet and was out the door in a minute, thinking something was wrong.

Jake, Matt and Mr. Tyree sat on the lawn, with puppies playing all over their laps. Mama dog lay nearby, watching. The three women stopped on the porch steps.

Casey was the first to speak. "Matt, we've been over that ground. Jake thinks it will be a cinch giving up a pup when it comes time to go, but I don't think it will be that easy for him." She didn't look in Jake's direction, knowing the face he would be making.

Matt's eyes crinkled at the corners. He grinned and looked to his father for support. "Every boy needs a dog, don't you agree?"

Mr. Tyree nodded enthusiastically. "You bet. Matthew's had dogs since he was a baby."

Theresa touched Casey's arm. "You sure you'll be leaving?" She zoned in on the only words she seemed to hear.

"Yes, I was telling you inside that we couldn't stay here in the winter. The cabin is a little too rustic and—"

"Oh, but they could stay in the main house, couldn't they?"

Matthew's mouth tightened. "Casey and I have discussed this. It's settled. They don't have to go far. I'm hoping she'll decide to stay in Parker to be near a clinic for Jake."

Casey avoided looking at Jake who she knew held out hope they could stay on the ranch. It was clear Matt didn't want the responsibility of two more people in his life. "There are things I can do there that I can't do here. Have you heard of Heart's Desire? They have one at Parker and also Center City. We could move there too, it doesn't have to be Parker." She looked at Matt as if to say, you can't decide for me.

He frowned and started to speak, but didn't.

"Heart's Desire? Of course, I've heard of it, and a wonderful idea it is too. Tom and I've gone to many functions to help raise money for it."

The women descended the steps to the yard to sit in lawn chairs. The puppies ran over to them and the golden one seemed to know just what to do, for he tumbled toward her, picking her out from all the others sitting there.

She saw Matt nudging Jake on the shoulder when the pup leaped into her lap. "I volunteered at a clinic in Phoenix and I miss working with the kids. In fact I thought what a wonderful opportunity it would be for the kids to come out here. Experience firsthand a ranch with horses and dogs and puppies along with clean, fresh air and good cooking." She refused to glance in Matt's direction, sure that he looked like a thundercloud.

Theresa clapped her hands together. "Oh my, what a splendid idea! Isn't it, Tom? Why didn't we think of that?"

Mr. Tyree didn't speak for a moment and everyone seemed to wait, hardly breathing. "Great! Good for you for thinking of it, Casey. It never occurred to us, as much as we've always tried to help the kids financially."

"Hold on a minute here," Matt interjected. "I thought I told Casey it wasn't practical, but maybe I didn't get that far with the conversation. The insurance would be out of this world, even though she claims the hospital has insurance. What if something happened to one of the kids? A horse could step on a foot, or someone could climb a tree and fall. Sixty miles might not seem a long way, but it would be in an emergency. I said I'd consider it, but I thought the conversation was closed."

"Oh pooh. Leave it to Matthew to put a blanket on a fire." Theresa looked at her son with less than delight. "You drag around here like it's the end of the world and every day you wake up is a mistake. I'm sick and tired of that attitude, young man. And don't go pouty on me as if I shouldn't talk in front of people. Casey and Jake are like family. I could see that right away."

Pouty? Casey hid a smile behind her hand. His mother had clearly told him off and he sat there and took it. On the other hand, what else could he do? Casey wondered if she would be like that with Jake when he was thirty-something. Without a doubt, she would.

"Your mother's right, Matt," Mr. Tyree enthused. "We could let them bring a few kids at a time to start with, to see if it works. Heckfire, I reckon your mom and me, we might even come back and stay for something like that. At least in the summer. We could fix up the bunkhouses. They are real sturdy and well-made. Wouldn't take much of a woman's touch to whip them in shape for visitors."

Theresa got up and paced back and forth in excitement. "Can't you just see the kids in bunk beds? They could eat breakfast over a fire some mornings, out of tin plates. Oh my Lord, they would be ecstatic."

"Paco and I would love it too," Carmela said. "It would be so good to hear children's voices around the place again." She looked in Jake's direction. "Not that Jake is not company. Still, he is but one little boy and does not stay with us for the most part."

Matt glared at the lot of them. "Well, if all of you are going to be so danged caught up in the idea, guess we'll have to. But I still don't think it's practical."

Casey smiled. "We'd just have to make inquiries. See if the board of directors at the clinic and the parents would give their permission. It's not like it will happen tomorrow."

The pups ran up and started playing under their feet.

"Which pup did you pick, Jake?" Mr. Tyree asked.

Casey started to protest and then thought better of it. Now wasn't the time. No one considered the sadness Jake would feel when he had to leave the puppy behind, but mothers had to think of all the factors in an action. Still maybe the fun of having his own puppy even for a short time would make Jake happier than not having one at all.

"Can't you tell, Mom? It's this one. He already loves us both." The yellow ball of fur stayed close to Jake while the other puppies romped and played on their mother.

"I suppose you named him already? Is it a him?" Casey asked.

"It's a male. I checked," Mr. Tyree said.

"I'm gonna think about the name." Jake's forehead wrinkled with the seriousness of his responsibility. "Might take me awhile," he drawled.

They laughed at his mimic of Matt's speech.

"Can I show him to Carmela? She went inside the house."

"Sure thing. But take him around to the back door. Carmela's a fanatic about that house and you wouldn't want to get on her bad side."

"As if he could," Theresa said.

They watched Jake run off, holding the puppy carefully in his arms.

"Come on, woman, let's look around the place," Mr. Tyree stood, stretched and reached his hand for his wife.

"We'll see you two later." They walked off toward the corral.

"I want to show you something, Casey," Matt said, unwinding his long frame from the chair he sat in. He motioned toward the Jeep in the driveway.

"I should tell Jake."

"We won't be long. He'll be talking about that pup for an hour and won't even miss us. We need to talk."

CHAPTER 19

They climbed into the Jeep and without a word of explanation, he headed down the rutted road toward Dorothy's house. They didn't speak. His jaw was set, his muscles working as they did when he was troubled. When he turned the car into the driveway, he pulled over, shifting his body so he faced her. "I've been wanting to tell you something."

For a moment, Casey felt as if the blood pumping through her veins had slowed to a mere dribble. Everything she looked at seemed to move in slow motion. Birds soared overhead, trees rustled in the slight breeze, all at half speed. Matt was going to tell her their lovemaking was a grievous mistake, and he wanted them to be just good friends.

Wasn't this the kiss-off women usually gave men? It wasn't fair. It made her efforts to win him over doubly hard. She knew—even if he didn't—that he needed her. He never said he loved her, true enough. Was it only sex he needed from her?

His expression remained tight and strained. "What happened between us on the mesa was..." He ran his hand distractedly through his hair, struggling for the right words.

Casey couldn't have helped him even if she wanted to. What was he trying to say?

"It was incredible," he continued. "I've grown attached to Jake. He's a good boy and you've done a heck of a job raising him. Even if I do think you coddle him."

The hint of a smile lurked around his lips, and his dark eyes caressed her face, causing her breath to catch as she looked at him.

"I've been thinking we should get married. It's the only realistic way you two can stay here and be safe. Everything would work out that way."

"What?" The sweet, soft feeling she had for him evaporated with the flood of disappointment sweeping over her from head to toe.

"I've thought it all out," he rushed to say. "You wouldn't have to leave here for the winter. You and Jake would have people to take care of you. Between Carmela and me, we know enough about doctoring to help Jake in any emergency. Truthfully, I don't believe his future holds many emergencies because he's doing so well."

He must have finally noticed Casey's change of expression and a look of confusion came over his face.

"You have the presumption to offer marriage because it's convenient?" Her voice tilted up and she struggled to keep it even. "We made love once and from that you surmise that I need a husband and Jake needs a father?"

She had gradually processed his words through a hazy blur of anger and frustration. The words of his emotionless, matter-of-fact marriage proposal finally sank in. She had expected courting, a tiny mention of love or affection, something to tell her he cared for her or needed her—something that said she was special.

His proposal was like a business deal. She would perform her wifely duties in exchange for room and board and security. That was actually what he said in so many words.

Dismay and disbelief turned to outrage, which quivered in her voice, causing it to fluctuate in that annoying manner. She had to stop in the middle of her explosion to take a deep breath.

That gave him a chance to recoup his usual air of confidence. He reached to touch her arm, to stop her flow of words. "We get along well, and our sex life would be fantastic." He grinned, obviously trying to keep it light. "I wouldn't mind a house filled with kids running around—brothers and sisters to Jake."

Casey jerked away from his touch. "You are beyond belief. A damned Neanderthal if I ever met one. What makes you so sure Jake and I need taking care of?" Beneath her anger, a sense of loss crept in. He couldn't love her. Not if he proposed marriage in this manner, like a convenient set-up, useful to everyone, freeze dried and separated from emotion. The word love was not a part of his vocabulary. "Haven't you ever heard of marrying for love?" She asked the question, striving for calm.

His open, honest expression showed puzzlement. "I—I hadn't thought of it," he admitted.

"No." Casey leaped out of the Jeep and paced at the side, her hair flying about her shoulders, her body trembling. She needed self-righteous anger to keep away the ache deep inside. "Your whole idea is ridiculous."

If she married him under these circumstances, if he never learned to love her, she would wither up and die. Or she would have to leave him eventually and Jake would be devastated. It would never work. He was incapable of loving anymore. His heart still lay inside that house.

She took a deep breath and slid back in the opened car door. "No." She felt the single spoken word fill the inside of the car leaving no room to breathe.

"I thought about your idea of kids coming here to the ranch. We could work that out."

"Don't use that as blackmail. It won't work. I can help the kids on my own if I have to."

He turned back to the wheel, his big hands tightening so that the steering wheel was in danger of snapping off.

It was then Casey noticed the pale strip of skin on his finger where his wedding band used to be. He had been so sure of her answer he removed the ring. That made her even angrier.

"I just thought...what's so bad about offering someone a comfortable life with loyalty and companionship? I'll always be there for you."

"Matt, I need love. I'm still young. I have a life ahead of me—I hope. I'm not going to marry for comfort or for security. I did that once." She had married Richard for what she thought were those very reasons. Stability and safety, she saw that now. The stability turned out to be stifling and barren—as false as their life together. She wouldn't make that mistake again. She didn't feel damaged any longer by the abandonment of her parents or leaving Richard. The idea gradually sunk in that she had managed to overcome her past and accepting this marriage of convenience would push her all the way back again. She didn't want to start from friendship and take a chance his love would blossom. What if it didn't? What if the chains he had cast on himself could not be broken?

"I'll welcome a comfortable, safe relationship about forty or fifty years from now." Casey thumped her chest with her fist. "But now I want undying love. I want the excitement of romance. I want to be courted and—"

"You mean wined and dined and flowers and a honeymoon? That's for teenagers. I don't have time for that."

She brushed away his words impatiently. "You make my wishes and needs sound trifling and unimportant. But they are not frivolous to me. I want a man who will make me feel special. I need a man who isn't afraid to show his love. If you have to ask what I mean, then you are truly hopeless. Such a waste."

Can't you say you love me just once? Can't you spare just a few gentle words of tenderness to show you care? Is that so hard? It would only be hard to say, if you don't love me.

Casey's voice softened, and all the while her heart felt as if the big Jeep had run over it a couple of times on the highway. Road kill, that's what it was. "I love you, Matt. It's that simple. I'm not afraid to say it. I said it once before but apparently you didn't notice. If you can't love me back, there's no hope for us."

He had turned his face away, looking out the window but he turned back to her, his eyes angry, closed against her, his lips a thin line. "I offered you the best I had to give and you threw it back in my face. Why do you need the words? What difference can a few words make when you don't want what I have to give?"

She shook her head. "You'll never understand, not in a lifetime. Not in a million years."

"Well," he moved away from her. "That says it all, then."

"Yes, it does. Take me back to the house, please. I don't know why you brought me out here anyway."

He wasn't finished "I need someone to ride the river with. You need someone to sweep you up and sail away with you on a pirate's ship. You'll have to grow up sooner or later, Casey. Life isn't like that."

She didn't want him to draw her into any more discussion. He must have brought her out here to Dorothy's house to show her that the exorcised ghost no longer inhabited his life. If he could propose to another woman, he must have finally cut Dorothy away or so he thought. But it wasn't true, was it? She was still a part of his life.

"You actually planned all this out before you brought me here to tell me?"

He shrugged, his expression showing honest confusion. "I thought you'd..."

"You thought I was dying on the vine at the ripe old age of thirty-something and you'd rescue me and give Jake a father all in one swoop of kindness? You wanted to tie it all up in one neat little package." Her lips curled in anger, to keep her breaking heart from showing and to hold the tears at bay.

"Maybe that's some of it," he admitted.

"Damn it! I don't want my life folded into a neat little package. We don't need anyone. Jake and I, we don't need charity."

Matt took hold of her arm in a tight grip that made her wince. His voice was harsh, his expression intense. "Woman, I wasn't offering you charity. I offered you a partnership in a life together."

Where his hand touched her, she felt electric sensations dig into her skin. Oh, God, she loved this big oaf of a man, but she would not—could not—settle for less than the whole package. If she accepted his proposal under these circumstances, she might win a corner of his life and she could also lose big time. If he never came to love her—if he never could give her anything of himself but companionship and sex—it just wasn't enough to build on. She would stay by his side through the years ahead and wither away inches by inches, loving him so badly. It would destroy her.

She pulled away. "You don't have a romantic bone in your body. And I'm not *settling*. As far as I am concerned, this conversation is finished. Let's go."

Both of them were silent all the way back to the ranch house.

Matt sat on the corral fence, staring at the placidly eating horses, contemplating where he went wrong. He never got a chance to show Casey the empty house.

To hell with it!

Women. He thought she would be happy at the idea of a good home for her and Jake. Sometimes she looked so lost, in spite of that mile wide chip on her shoulder.

He wanted to take care of her, to protect her. More than that, he wanted to lie at her side every night and wake up looking at that glorious hair spread out on a pillow every morning.

Why didn't she know that without him having to put it all in words? Because she wanted something different than he knew how to give her. She didn't want him, she made that damn clear.

He remembered his words about Casey wanting a pirate's ship to sail away on. To hell with riding the river with her. He wanted her in the saddle with him, leaning against him through all the years to come.

But it was clear she didn't want him.

CHAPTER 20

The elder Tyrees left, promising to come back soon. Matt stayed out on the range mending fences, just coming in to eat. He and Casey avoided speaking if possible. When it was time to take Jake to Parker, Carmela offered to come along.

"Thanks, but we'll be home in a few days. Maybe we'll stay a week to see what's going on, take in a movie or two." She needed time to herself without Carmela and Paco looking from Matt to her and back again, knowing something was wrong.

The visit to the doctors went well. Jake's heart proved healthy and his asthma symptoms had nearly disappeared. The doctors told Casey that Jake would be safe in the cold climate, even in the Colorado winter as long as she took sensible precautions. Some of their suggestions made Casey smile. Didn't they think she had a brain in her head? She thought of the litany of don'ts. Don't go out in a blizzard, stay warm and dry. All very good advice if she were staying in Colorado.

Casey asked questions about Heart's Desire from some of the nurses and she and Jake spent some time visiting the floor where the kids were hospitalized. On the second day, she met Helen from the park at the nurse's station. It was her duty day and she showed Casey around and took Jake in to meet the kids.

He ran to each bed in turn and chattered away with the children, as if he had known them all his life. That might be a sign Jake needed the companionship of children his own age.

Matt seemed to think she already decided to stay in Parker, but Casey hadn't made up her mind yet. She could rent an apartment or a house for her and Jake and then volunteer her time when she wasn't writing. Jake could go to public school. Somehow, Casey didn't think the idea of staying only sixty miles from Matt would work. What if he came to see her? What if he wanted to make love again? Could she turn him down flat? She and Jake would be better off moving far away, to another state.

They went to a movie and she took Jake to the zoo. "I had planned for us to stay here a few days, but I'd rather not. How about you?"

The blissful look on his face told her he was ready to leave anytime. When they were packed and ready to go, he seemed anxious to get home.

"I miss my puppy," Jake said on the way home. "I named him Duke because Matt said that was his hero's name when I asked him did he have a hero."

"Hmm. That's nice, dear." Why didn't it surprise her that John Wayne would be Matt's hero? How was she going to tell Jake they had to move soon and far away? If she could manage to take the puppy with them, that would soften the blow somewhat. But not knowing where she would go and under what circumstances she would live, it wouldn't be convenient to worry about a pup too. Damn Matt, she warned him not to give Jake a dog.

Carmela and Paco met them in the circular drive where they stopped before going on to their cabin. Casey struggled to hide her disappointment, expecting to see the tall, angular frame of Matt at least in the background somewhere.

Jake leaped out of the car, running toward Carmela. "I'm good! The doctors say I'm 'bout well." He laughed as Carmela lifted him off his feet, squeezing him.

Casey saw Paco turn away, his dark eyes suspiciously bright with tears as Carmela opened her arms to receive Casey, too.

Matt came around the corner of an outbuilding, a little ball of fur following him, and Casey's heart did a pirouette.

Jake forgot his hero for a moment as he swooped the puppy up in his arms. "Hey, pard. I missed you. We're gonna be okay, did you hear?"

"I'm happy for you both." Matt looked as if he wanted to put his hand on her shoulder as he used to do, but he turned to talk to Jake.

Casey watched them a moment while Carmela chatted on.

"I'll follow you down the hill, make sure everything's okay in the cabin," Matt said.

"Oh no, you don't have to bother. We know the way by now."

He had that withdrawn, stubborn look in his eyes. "You've been living in the main house and it's been awhile since you stayed in the cabin. I'll make sure no porcupines have settled in and that you have firewood. Nights are getting nippy."

When both vehicles pulled up in front of the cabin, Jake jumped out and put down the puppy. "This is home, Duke. But mind, it's only temporary."

Both of them ran around the grounds, in and out of trees, up and down the porch steps. It felt good not having to caution Jake to slow down and she could tell Matt enjoyed Jake's laugher and the pup's antics as much as she enjoyed watching them.

Matt drew her aside and touched her shoulder, pointing toward the mountains. "Don't want to scare you, but I wouldn't let the pup out without Jake or someone with him. He might wander off."

"You are talking about the puma, aren't you?" They whispered to keep the sounds from Jake.

"Maybe. The animals are safe up at the ranch. A puma would never come near with all the activity and human and dog smells. But this cabin is isolated. If I thought there was danger to Jake, I would have said something, but I am one hundred percent sure the cat wouldn't come here either. But if the pup wandered off..."

"Thank you for the warning. I'll make sure Jake understands." She turned away, missing the warming touch of his hand on her shoulder. As she stepped up onto the porch, he walked over to where Jake and the dog played.

Keep it light, she ordered herself. "Hey you guys, I'm for making us hamburgers and fries. Anyone up for that?"

Matt regarded her quizzically for a moment. "You sure?"

"Of course, Matt. We're friends, aren't we?"

A sardonic smile lurked at the corner of his lips. She wanted to kiss him so badly at the moment. Moving her gaze from his mouth to his eyes, she was startled to see the banked fires deep inside. His desire for her had not changed. So she had to be strong.

Would he tell Jake about his proposal and her refusal? If he did, Jake would be broken hearted. He would never understand or forgive her.

While they ate the hamburgers and fries, Casey waited for the damning words from Matt. She expected them when Jake stopped speaking, asked to be excused from the table, and ran off outside with his puppy.

"I appreciate you not telling him—about us."

Matt shook his head. "Good Lord, woman. Give me some credit. Jake and I, we have a buddy thing going, but you are his whole life. I'd never tell him you turned me down flat."

Their lovemaking had been so passionate, so rich, so exciting. The memory of their bodies twined, with his hands roaming at will, touching secret places made her skin warm to remember. Did he think of this, too?

She looked into his eyes, and realized he was trying to tell her that the proposal still stood. He was too proud to offer again, and for that she was relieved. She was only so strong.

It was masculine ego, and any hurt he felt, he was sure to get over. She hoped she would be so lucky. Now they *had* to go away for the winter. Staying here would prove nothing and could be a hardship for everyone.

"Let's go to Parker again," Casey said one morning. It had been a week since she had seen Matt. The first few days dragged by so slowly, but she was more and more certain she had made the right decision.

"To the doctor?" Jake wanted to know.

Casey shook her head. "Just for a trip. I need to check the mail and we could go to a show, get a pizza."

Jake hadn't asked about Matt after the first few days when it was obvious he wasn't dropping in for a visit. How could she possibly explain it to Jake? She would just have to wait until they were ready to move and do it then.

On their way out, they stopped by the main house and Jake handed over the pup to Paco's care. He wanted to take him along, but knew that wouldn't work out.

They didn't talk much on their way to Parker. Casey was content listening to the radio and Jake played his video games. When they arrived, they ate lunch at the soda fountain, so Jake could have a root beer float. Afterward they went to pick up the mail.

As soon as Casey touched the long white envelope, she felt an ominous heaviness in the pit of her stomach. She moved her fingers over the raised lettering of the return address of an attorney. A lawyer with a Central City address, a very bad sign.

"Jake, honey, wait for me in the car. I have to get some stamps." As soon as he left, she hurriedly tore into the envelope. It was worse than she could have imagined. The Nichols had hired an attorney to force her to allow them the right to monitor and help with Jake's health issues. The overriding factors in their affidavit was her lack of a job to support herself, being so far from a public or private school and the Nichols' considerable resources compared to hers.

Casey leaned against the cold marble wall of the post office for support. She was determined not to run to Matt with this problem. Their relationship had been relegated to that of friendship just now. If she told him about this letter, he would insist that he was right, that being married would solve all her problems. Or even worse, he would turn away because she hurt his pride by her adamant refusal.

There had to be another way.

Outside, the bright sunlight warred with her inner gloom. Jake was waiting in the car, watching people pass by. "I want to make a call and then we can go to the park. Maybe you'll see David. Remember him?"

"Yaay!" Jake shouted, raising his arms in the air and kicking his feet against the floorboard.

The best thing she could do would be to confront this Center City attorney face to face. He didn't have authority to take Jake away, as far as she knew. They had to be bluffing. At that moment, she despised her in-laws more than anyone in her life for causing this shadow over their lives when they were trying to start fresh.

"I think we'll go to home, pack a few things, and then head for Center City in the morning, stay overnight." Taking out her cell phone, she called the attorney and managed to persuade his secretary to give her an appointment in two days. Now all she had to do was come up with the appropriate words to convince the man that she had the right to care for Jake and that the Nichols were wrong.

Jake needed a little outside time and she wanted to sit and think away from people, so they went to the park near the hospital.

Jake played on the swings for a while. Casey could tell he was losing interest when David ran toward him. Thank goodness, Helen and her son had decided to come to the park just then. Casey needed someone to talk to, to bounce her ideas off of.

"Hi, Helen. I was hoping to see you again."

The tall, willowy brunette smiled and sat down on the bench beside her. "What's up? You look as if you've been dragged through a knot hole."

"Thanks. I needed that." They both laughed

Casey reached inside her purse and brought out the letter. "Ever heard of this lawyer?"

Helen frowned at the return address and shook her head. "Why?"

"My ex in-laws have hired him to find a way to get part time custody of Jake."

"Don't you already share him with your ex?"

"No. He never asked for visiting rights. He's probably started another family by now.'

"Bummer. Why do you suppose the grandparents are concentrating on Jake?"

"To be truthful, I think it's the name. He is Richard Jacob the Third. How I wish I had named him Jeremy or Stephen or Archibald, I don't care what. The Colonel, that's Mr. Nichols, wants an heir. He is fanatical about it. I don't think my ex ever confided in them that he didn't care about Jake."

"And they think they can give Jake more than you? How about it? Do they have the money and the power to bestow instant health?"

Casey dug her booted toe into the dirt under the swing, and then she stopped. That was Matt's thing, digging his boot in the dirt when he was distressed or puzzled. "Of course not. The doctors say the asthma will probably run its course in time. All this fresh air and exercise has done wonders. They think I need to show I can support him, other than by Richard's checks, that is."

Helen smacked her palm against her thigh. "We always need help on the floor. Instead of volunteering, I bet you could get at least a part time job at the hospital. You would have day care for Jake and soon you can enroll him in school. That will take up most of his day. It would prove you can take care of your family."

"It's an idea, but not that simple. A judge may look at the Nichols and think they should at least share in his life."

"Is that such a bad thing?"

"It wouldn't be, if Jake liked them. But the Colonel terrifies him. He intimidates the heck out of me, too. I've never said a word against either one of them to Jake, but still—"

"Your son probably senses how you feel."

"I'm sure he does. I know that's not fair. Under any other circumstances, I'd be glad to let them share in his life. I've never been convinced that *they* want to share. They could take him away from me. Money is power."

Helen sighed. They didn't speak for a few moments while they watched their boys playing on the grass. "I know I'm off the subject, but have you thought any more about Heart's Desire? You did mention you were interested when I was here and also in Center City."

Casey didn't want to tell her new friend quite yet that they might move out of Colorado, so she only nodded.

"Great! Then maybe you could help us out sometime. We seldom get seasoned volunteers. Just yesterday, a fifteen year old came in with leukemia. It's in remission, and he just finished a course in chemo. It's so damned sad. His parents live out in the boonies, on a ranch fifty or sixty miles away and can't get in to visit but every other week."

"Is the boy angry?" That was one of the stages. The worst to deal with was the resignation stage. The kids got to that part before the parents were able to.

"He's past the anger. His parents are bitter though. He's their only child. I don't know how parents cope. The kids are usually tougher. Maybe it's because they don't quite understand-you know, the finality of death—all that."

Casey put her hand on Helen's arm. "I'll be there one way or another. It might be good for Jake to visit them. He's learning computers. He could teach them. He draws and paints, too."

"Well, there you are. If you tell this to a lawyer, he'd understand more about you and Jake. See that you guys are okay." Something in her voice didn't sound as convinced as her words.

"You still think the Nichols' money could win out?"

Helen shrugged. "Who can say, at this point? Don't go in with a closed mind. You say your appointment is in the afternoon. I work the night shift. I can watch Jake for you."

"Thanks, but I think the lawyer should see Jake. See for himself what a normal kid he is."

After checking her watch, Helen got up to go. "I'll hold you to your promise about Heart's Desire, I warn you. It'd be good for you and the kids sure need you."

"I'll give it a lot of thought," Casey assured her.

She and Jake watched Helen and David leave. How wonderful would it be for this fifteen-year-old boy to visit a ranch, to talk to a horse and pet puppies? Her idea was good, she knew it was, but she couldn't help put it into effect if she wasn't there at the ranch and that wasn't going to happen. A pervasive sense of loss flooded her so that she was glad to be sitting on the park bench. Her legs might not have held her up.

The love she felt for Matt was unlike any she had imagined would ever come to her. But the love wasn't returned and that was so hard to accept. He didn't need anyone or want anyone. He was content with his life the way he lived it. She was pleased for him that he could be satisfied, but somewhere inside her gut, she thought he was not being true to himself. He was in denial and by the time he figured it out, she and Jake would be gone.

That night they went to the movies. Jake's new appetite never ceased to amaze her. In Phoenix, he had been indifferent to food. She'd had to coax him to eat at every meal. Glancing at him in the movie, she smiled to see him shoving buttered popcorn in his mouth as if he couldn't get it in there fast enough. Truly amazing.

When they left the movie and walked down the street, he was still eating. Talking around a mouthful, he whispered, "Mom, did you and Matt bust up?"

"Hey, what did I tell you about talking with your mouth open?" That had never failed to tickle him when she said that.

"You mean full," he corrected her, as he always did.

"Matt and I were never serious so there's no busting up involved. We were—are friends. He's busy now, something about cows and fences."

"You're supposed to call them cattle."

"Oh yeah, sorry."

"Matt says only tourists say cows. Are we tourists? What's a tourist?"

She smiled at his seriousness. "It's kind of an old-fashioned word for traveler, like those who go around visiting interesting places. Like Mr. and Mrs. Tyree. No, I don't think we would qualify as tourists." It was a good time to ask him.

"What do you think about living in Parker or Center City for the winter? Maybe we could go back to the cabin for the summer, but I can't promise. It depends."

Jake shook his head, his mouth straightened in a stubborn look. "Why can't we stay at Matt's ranch?"

She didn't want to make up stories to satisfy him, but there was just so much a six-year-old needed to know. "It's hard to explain, sweetie. A grown man and woman are not supposed to stay together if they aren't married." That sounded priggish and stuffy, but it wouldn't hurt him to learn a few values even at his early age.

His frown said he accepted her words, even though they didn't please him.

Casey figured she might as well level with him about his grandparents and the lawyer. She wanted him to go with her. Maybe the lawyer would be astute enough to recognize the bond she and Jake shared. She explained about her appointment and what she planned to say.

"Mom, you know I don't want to stay with anyone but you." Jake folded his arms across his chest and glared at her.

"Hey, don't get in an uproar. I'm just telling you what is happening so you can be prepared. We'll talk to the lawyer and listen to what he has to say."

"Well, I won't ever stay with them!"

"Mr. and Mrs. Nichols are your grandmother and grandfather, the only ones you are likely to have." He asked her once about her parents, his other grandma and grandpa. She explained as simply as she could at the time, thinking he wasn't ready for some heavy explanation.

His forehead wrinkled, and he wanted to say something, but lapsed into silence for a moment. "I don't think I probably need a grandma and grandpa," he finally said.

"Well, maybe not, but I never had any and I wouldn't wish that on you." He didn't look convinced, but she would have to wait and see what the new day would bring.

CHAPTER 21

They returned to the cabin, packed clothes and napped a few hours before heading back to Center City. She didn't see anyone from the big house so they were probably all still asleep or off working. By the time they got to Center City, the afternoon sun had disappeared. In its place, a glowering, cloudy sky promised rain and plenty of it. In the distance, Casey heard thunder rolling out from behind the mountains.

Jake had slept much of the time. She shook him awake when they arrived at the motel they had stayed in before. During the ride, she marshaled her thoughts. First, she needed to separate emotions from facts. Even so, there was no way Jake would be better off staying part time with her and part time with the Nichols. Or maybe stuck in some nursing environment to be picked over and inspected like a bag of old clothes in a rummage sale. It well could be that Richard's parents weren't just being vindictive, but truly thought their money could buy better care for their grandson. And as Richard had done, they had neglected the love quotient.

Looking up at the sky, she thought, how appropriate it was to have this kind of weather today. She held tight to Jake's hand as they crossed the street and walked up the few short steps to the attorney's office.

She gave her name and the receptionist asked her to wait. Casey patted her hair, which she had spent a lot of time trying to coax into a neat twist at the nape of her neck. Her navy blue jacket and skirt with a crisp white blouse were perfect. She felt at ease, if she discounted the occasional butterflies in her stomach. So much was at stake. She needed to remain calm and composed. No telling what the Nichols had told this man.

The room felt stuffy and over furnished, smelling of leather and furniture polish. She heard the whirring of computer equipment in the background above the soft music.

"Mom, do we got to do this?" Jake pulled at her sleeve and whispered.

She patted his knee and nodded. "Got to, son."

It took a while until the receptionist called them in. At fifteen minutes past her appointment time, the receptionist finally told them that Mr. Hennessy could see them. Casey recognized a power play when she saw one. The attorney had no other clients unless they had left by the back door.

When they were finally ushered in, the difference between the outer room and the inner sanctum was startling. The walls were bare, with only diplomas to mar their blankness. Stark, utilitarian furniture, and a huge desk completed the office furnishings.

Casey looked at the man seated behind the desk.

"Mrs. Nichols, Jacob, please sit." The attorney stood and motioned to chairs in front of the desk. "As you know, I'm Alexander Hennessy."

He was a tall, spare man, authoritative and stern looking. Casey felt at a disadvantage against his superior manner, as if she were back in high school with a visit to the principal. She crossed her legs at the ankles, held her sweaty palms together in a semi-loose clasp on her lap and tried her darndest to appear at ease.

"Good afternoon, Mr. Hennessy. Thank you for seeing us on such a short notice."

Without her needing to tell him, Jake sat.

"My clients don't wish to cause you problems," the attorney began without preamble. He sat down again with his elbows on his desk, the long, bony fingers of each hand touching at the tips. He leaned his chin on them, looking at her over half glasses.

She found it quite intimidating in a folksy sort of way and felt certain he must have practiced the look in a mirror until he had gotten it just right. She tried to picture him in his boxer shorts, for surely that was what he wore underneath that expensive-looking business suit. Would they be a pale blue to match his tie? She fought the smile that began at the corner of her lips. Now is not the time for frivolous thoughts, she told herself.

"Perhaps it's true, the Nichols don't mean to cause problems. However, they are doing it just the same. I have full custody of my son, given to me by the courts. His father never contested it, why should the grandparents?"

A bleak smile touched his lips. "I'm sure you know the answer to that. Colonel and Mrs. Nichols feel they can offer more financial opportunities. You have no permanent address, no job, and the only income you have is what your ex-husband gives you, which I understand is quite generous."

Aaargh! How she would like to do something physical, like throw a book at him or dump his paper clips out on his desk. She didn't dare, there was too much at stake.

"That may be true up to a point. I am going to make a permanent home either here in Center City or in Parker. I'm a writer and I earned a living at it before I met Jake's father. My editor let me know there is a strong demand for the type of writing I do. In the meantime, I plan to apply at the hospital for part time work while Jake is in school. I have had experience working with sick children and have a good chance of being hired. I've been told both the Parker Clinic and the hospital here in Center City need part time help desperately."

"Hmmm." He leaned back in his chair and regarded Jake with a solemn expression.

Bless his heart. She repressed a grin that threatened. Jake didn't fidget, but returned his stare eye for eye.

"We'll be a part of the community as soon as we move."

At his raised eyebrows, she rushed on. "I can obtain depositions from the doctors here and at Parker and probably back in Phoenix. Since Jake's doctor moved from Phoenix to Center City I have everything I need for Jake close by. He has improved one hundred percent since I removed him from the stressful environment created by the Nichols."

There was complete silence in the room, as if the air had been sucked out of it. Into the dead void, Jake's voice sounded squeaky and small, but he didn't stutter.

"I want to stay with my mom. I don't like Sir and I don't like Ma'am." Jake folded his skinny arms across his chest in that utterly masculine way that was usually so comical she always had to laugh. Not this time. His words brought tears to her eyes, her throat choked up so that she could not have spoken if she had wanted to.

"And why is that, son? Why don't you like your grandparents?" The attorney smiled graciously as if he really wanted to hear what Jake had to say.

Jake opened his mouth and then faltered. Casey knew he didn't want to bad-mouth his grandparents. She had taught him about respecting his elders and had always urged him to try to accept both of them as part of their family.

The boy took a deep breath, not looking in her direction. "My mom loves me. She doesn't 'spect me to do stuff. Stuff I don't want to do."

"Does Jacob go to school, Mrs. Nichols?"

He must know she home schooled Jake. "Not yet. We had satellite lessons in Phoenix. Here I tutor him. He'll be ready for school by the time we get settled this fall."

Mr. Hennessy shuffled papers, took off his glasses, put them back on and by then Casey knew he was not as self-assured as he had first appeared to be.

She thought that was a good sign—until there was a knock on the door and Richard and his parents walked into the room.

Casey felt as if someone kicked her in the stomach and she heard Jake draw in a sharp breath. The attorney looked smug as he walked around his desk to shake hands all around.

"Please. Take seats. Maybe we can get this all straightened out."

Casey looked at Richard. None of the old feelings came back, not even the anger and despair. He looked fit and somehow younger, maybe without his family to tie him down.

"Hello Casey. Long time. Looking good." He bent to touch her shoulder and she tried her best not to flinch away. "How's the big boy? I must say, you aren't the same fella who left Phoenix, are you?" His voice showed surprise and a tinge of approval.

He didn't offer to hug Jake or even shake his hand. In turn, Jake sat still, not quite knowing what to do.

"Neither of us are the same," Casey said. Did he want Jake back now that he appeared healthy?

"Ah—I'm sorry things turned out the way they did, but truthfully, I didn't expect you to run away and take Jake." He spoke as if they were the only two people in the room.

"Richard, you could have shown Jake a little affection once in a while. It wouldn't have made him a sissy, like you claimed it would."

"The Colonel never had to take that attitude with me and I turned out just fine."

That's certainly debatable. "Just because your father was such a strict disciplinarian, doesn't follow that you had to be."

"You mollycoddled the boy. Always have. Not good for him."

As time passed, Richard had started to talk like his father, barking out words with periods at the end of short sentences. That was part of his control thing, hard to argue with short, pithy sentences.

"I didn't expect visiting rights," Richard said. Although his tone was conversational, the words struck as practiced and rehearsed. "I'll give you all the financial help you need and of course support the boy. If you wanted a new life, you were free to start it. Neither one of you ever really needed me."

We never needed you because you were never there for us. "You have it all wrapped up with your cozy new life with Jennifer." She knew just when he met her, at the country club last year when she refused to go to a boring golf awards dinner. She'd heard rumors.

"There is no Jennifer. Let's not turn this into ugliness, Casey. That's not like you."

No, it had never been like her. She had accepted everything Richard handed out to her as if she couldn't do anything else. Her decision to leave astonished him, but he recovered quickly she noticed.

"You're not here to see me or Jake. You're here for your parents." Casey acknowledged the pair for the first time. "Your parents tried to smother Jake with kindness. They thought they knew the best treatment for his asthma and had the resources and money to prove it. If they had their way, he would be living with them at this very moment. Don't you think I know that?"

"We've never really spoken of it, my dear," Mrs. Nichols placated.

"It didn't matter how many times I've tried to talk to you about it. You always shut me out. I'm not against sharing Jake with you under certain circumstances. But the way you have bulldozed your ideas and wishes without considering Jake's feelings have left him cold to you. I certainly have never said anything against either you or Richard to my son."

The colonel, usually the one who talked first, seemed reticent next to Richard. As if he was taking a cue from him.

"Look, you can see Jake is one hundred percent better. I can show you records from Parker and Center City to prove that. What is it you came here for, Richard?"

He looked a little annoyed, whether at himself or her, she didn't know. It took him a while to answer and then he motioned toward the door. "Can we talk privately a moment?"

She didn't want to, but decided it was best to get it all out in the open and over with.

She followed him out to the hallway and he closed the door behind him. When he took hold of her arm, she pulled away.

"I guess I thought, well—maybe we could start over again as a family. But I can see you are so different."

He looked deep into her eyes and she wondered if he could tell she had made love to someone else. Oddly enough, that didn't bother her.

"Water under the bridge, Richard. Jake and I, we are, as you said, different people now. Our marriage didn't work and I accept some responsibility for not acting like an adult. I've faced up to the concept that I married you for my own lack of security and low self-esteem and wasn't helping our marriage any more than you were. We never really tried to salvage our marriage, but anything we did after a while was like putting a bandage on an open wound."

"I understand that I might have been a better husband and father. Maybe it's not in me."

He did look truly contrite and she put her hand on his arm. "Nonsense. You do take after your father and mother who are not the warmest people on earth, but you and I, in the beginning, had good times. You can have that again with someone. Just try to lighten up. As soon as I can get work, you can stop alimony payments. I'll put the support money for Jake in a college fund for him. Is that ok?"

"Sure. But don't worry about money. You know I have it."

She knew that, but the sooner they were entirely separate from him the better.

"I don't want Jake to go with your parents. It's true I've never badmouthed them to Jake, but he's terrified of your father."

Richard managed a grin. "Hell, I am too at times. I'll work it out with them. Maybe when you get settled they can come for a visit."

"Sure, that would work." She wanted to hug him goodbye for old time's sake, but he already turned away, pushing the door open.

"I guess that's it, then," he said as they entered the room and all eyes were on them with unspoken questions.

"I think Jake and I will leave now. We'll probably see you later but I'll keep in touch." Casey nodded toward Richard and his parents and took Jake's hand to leave.

The attorney cleared his throat and spoke. "I'll offer my recommendations to the Nichols. You'll hear from us." He stood, his manner politely dismissive, holding out his hand to her first and then Jake.

Casey felt as if she teetered on the edge of a precipice. Had she done everything possible to persuade the attorney? The Nichols were paying him—a major factor. In spite of their money, they didn't love and accept Jake for who he was and the person he would someday be. They wanted to possess him. She hoped she and Jake together had made the lawyer see this. She didn't see how a court could take Jake away from her, but it wasn't impossible. She hoped Richard would speak up for them when she left.

The storm that had threatened all day descended upon them when they walked out onto the sidewalk. The wind blew perpendicular, while the rain struck them like sharp little pieces of glass. She picked Jake up and rushed down the street, trying to outrun the force of the storm.

Inside their motel room, they laughed as her hair fell out of its constraints and tumbled around her face and shoulders. Jake ran into the bathroom to bring back towels.

Jake rubbed the towel through his wet hair. "Man, that's a lot of weather."

Where had he picked up that phrase? From Matt, no doubt. It sounded just like him.

Matt. Casey sat down on the bed, the laughter suddenly gone. He was out of their life. What would that do to Jake? Surely, he hadn't been around Matt long enough that it would make a hole in his life. Like it would with her.

"I didn't have to go with Richard?" Jake finally squeaked out the question that he had obviously been waiting to ask.

"No. Or the Nichols. However, I think someday soon they can come for a one-day visit. We might grow to like them. I bet the Colonel has lots of great war stories to tell."

The attorney seemed to have made a decision regarding Jake. She could only pray it was in their favor. The Nichols probably wouldn't give up that easily though. She would hear from them again. If they would just back off, she wouldn't mind them being involved in Jake's life. But they wanted all of him. They had already told her they didn't see any point in sharing him.

The sooner she started making her new life, the better. If it hurt too much to be as close as Parker or Center City to where Matthew lived, she could always move somewhere else, farther away, later. The next step was to get back to the cabin and pack.

CHAPTER 22

Back in the cabin, being so much closer to Matt, made Casey bitterly unhappy. She worked on her book to ease the pain until they left. Jake insisted they put more notes in the tumbleweeds so he drew pictures and she made little four line bits of poetry, but her heart wasn't in it. If Matt found them, he would just think her foolish.

The skies darkened early now, the days shorter, while thick clouds drifted in from behind the mountains, portending the winter weather.

"Mom, I need to interrupt you."

Jake stood next to her chair, that wonderful earnest look on his face.

"Okay, shoot."

"If we gotta go before winter, can we at least wait to the first snow? I'd like to see some snow."

"You've seen snow before. Remember when we lived in Phoenix? I took you to Flagstaff one winter." Now that she thought about it, he might have been too small to remember. "We'll see plenty of snow in Parker or Center City."

"I told Matt I saw snow before, but he said that was tame snow."

Casey laughed and tousled his hair. "Nut! Snow's snow."

When had he spoken to Matt? She hadn't seen him since they came back from the city. Probably in one of their earlier conversations, they'd had one of their man-talk things.

"Well, can we wait?" Jake wasn't one to get side-tracked.

"I can't promise, sweetie. We'll have to see what the weather picture looks like. We could be snowed in for weeks if we linger too long and the first snow is a heavy one." The fleeting satisfied look on his face told her the thought had occurred to him.

She pulled him closer and gave him a hug. "We might come back next summer if you want. Maybe. No promises, mind you. We just can't stay alone here in the cabin, in case we need something. There won't be electricity without the sun panels."

Jake ran to his room to bring out a picture of his puppy. He hadn't asked about his puppy yet. That made her feel so sad. He had resigned himself to not having it on a permanent basis. How many little boys would understand that? The idea gave her small comfort. She wanted him to stay a child for as long as it took him to grow up, not rush things.

The picture Jake had drawn was of a laughing puppy, tongue lolling out, with wide round eyes. "That looks just like Duke," she said.

"I want to put it in the tumbleweeds. Do you have something too?"

Casey had written a poem just after they got back from the city, but now the idea felt juvenile, from Matt's point of view, putting it in a bush. She visualized the neat little stack of notes on his desk. Why had he kept them?

Normally she would have confronted Matt, asked why he kept the notes, but Carmela had begged her not to mention it. That was odd. Why should it matter? He didn't strike her as an autocratic boss to work for. Carmela seemed to do as she pleased around the ranch house, more like a loved and respected member of the family.

"I don't know if I have anything to put in there. It really doesn't make much sense to throw words away."

"But you never said you was throwing words away."

"Were. Were throwing words away," she corrected absent-mindedly.

Was it throwing words away? What was so different in sending out a message not knowing if anyone would ever see it and sending one out with the off-chance that Matt would read it? Sighing, she pulled out her poem.

"Really, mom? You have one to send? Put your paper next to mine."

Casey drew on her leather gloves and picked up a tumbleweed from their stash behind the porch. She loved Matt so much, loved him too much to watch her life ripped to shreds because it started out as a one-sided love and never changed. Matthew had no room in his life except for his memories. She needed more. Even if she never found another man to love her or share her life, that would be better than sharing a tiny corner of his life with him, knowing there was more, but she just couldn't reach it.

It wasn't fair to Jake either. Jake loved Matt and she knew he cared for her son. One day Jake would be out of the nest, on his own. How lonely would her life be then? Even great sex lost its luster over time, without love to keep it shiny.

She pushed the papers way inside and threw the tumbleweed off in the next gust of wind where it danced a little jig all the way down the incline toward its final destination.

"Do they crumble up and the notes blow away?" Jake asked

That was kind of a logical, grown-up question. Until now he seemed content believing that someone eventually found and read them.

"It's like the bottle I told you about that people sometimes throw in the ocean. The chances of someone finding the note inside is maybe a million to one. The fun is in putting in the message and the fantasy of never knowing if someone read it."

"Maybe we should put our name and address on the paper. Then we could know."

She shook her head. "Wouldn't work. We'd lose the adventure right there. For example, what if this eighty-year-old prospector with a long white beard and a mustache stained with chewing tobacco comes riding up on a sway back mule someday and says, 'Is this here the place where they're throwin' out pictures of roadrunners and puppies?' Phooey, and he would take a big spit off the porch. He might decide to stay with us and never leave."

Jake began to giggle and then broke out in laughter as he formed the picture in his mind.

She joined him and they laughed until tears rolled down their cheeks. Unexpectedly he turned to her and threw his arms around her neck.

"I love you, Mom." He didn't stay still but for a moment, but that was enough for Casey. She swallowed hard, feeling like a traitor for not accepting Matt's offer so that Jake would have a father to love, too. "I want to walk up to see Duke. All by myself." His look challenged her.

"You're getting big now. I suppose you could walk up the road to the main house." Matt had told her the puma would never come close to the buildings and she trusted his judgment. Jake needed to have her trust him, too. "Why don't you bring Duke down for a few days or however long we're here?" Seeing the look of absolute joy on his face made her want to cry. "Wait a minute. You have to promise not to beg or whine or cry when we have to leave Duke behind. Can you do that? He'll be fine with his mother."

"Matt said he was giving the brothers and sisters away to other ranchers." Jake was still a moment, the light went out of his eyes and then it returned in the way little boys had of changing their thoughts so quickly. "I promise. I want to tell him goodbye."

"You can stay two hours if you like, but no more, or I'll worry. It will be a good time to visit with Paco and Carmela too. Ask Carmela when two hours are up. And stay on the road, don't go wandering."

"Aw, Mom. Maybe I'll see Matt."

"Don't count on it. He's busy getting things ready for the first blizzard."

Casey watched as Jake trudged up the roadway. She could imagine puma's lunging from the brush or him twisting his ankle on a stone in the path or not finding the pup when he got to the house, but a part of her knew it was time to back off and let him go.

The first snowfall two days later took Casey by surprise. Each day the sky had been open and blue then all of a sudden a strong, chill wind had blown in low scudding clouds with a distinct, clinging smell of snow.

Not a half hour later, the wind died away, the temperature turned a little warmer, and big soft flakes began to sift down from the sky. Casey and Jake ran outside to stand in the middle of the front yard.

"Shut your eyes, turn your face up, and hold out your arms," Casey said.

Jake did as she asked, laughing with his face turned up, waiting with eyes closed.

"Feel the snow kisses?" she asked. She couldn't tear her eyes away from his face, so trusting and open. He seemed to have grown taller since they'd come to Colorado and he no longer had that gaunt, old man look.

"I wish Matt could be here with us. How come he thinks we have to leave when it snows? Doesn't he want to be with us?"

Casey closed her eyes and turned her own face up to receive the soft blessing of the new snow.

Matthew. The name twisted something inside her middle. She knew when they left here it would be finished. She longed to feel his touch once more, oh God, only once more. Those strong hands, gently stroking, touching, feeling, and the mind-numbing fire that sped through her body. The soaring feeling of leaping over that mystic wall for the first time in her life.

"Mom, you're crying. Is it because you like our first snow?"

Casey brushed away the tears on her sleeve and nodded, unable to speak. She had tried to teach Jake that it was okay to be moved to tears by something wonderful as well as something sad. "The first snow is always special. But it also means it's time to think seriously about leaving soon." She took his hand and they walked up the incline toward the porch steps.

"After this comes the real stuff. The dark, low clouds that stay around for days and bring wind-driven blizzards." She felt goose bumps on her arms thinking what a pleasure those kinds of days would be to spend with Matt. They would cuddle on the couch, wrapped in an afghan and watching the fire in the fireplace. The cozy picture splintered into pieces and she blinked her eyes to get rid of the image. "What if we had an emergency?"

"Yeah. Like when Matt took me to the clinic. We were sure scared, weren't we?"

"I'm not trying to scare you, but I just need you to understand why we have to go."

"We got lots of wood," he offered. He let the puppy down and Duke yapped at each snowflake that landed on his nose.

She patted his hand absently. "I know, sweetheart, I know. But it's not a good idea." She didn't want to take it too far, but he had to know the decision had not come easy and it was final. That was probably a hard concept for a six-year-old to understand.

They sat on the porch swing, Jake holding the puppy, and watched the thickening soft white cover the ground. She wanted so badly to hear from the attorney and yet she feared it. Either way, a letter from him would decide her and Jake's future.

"We won't ever come back here, will we?" His voice trembled and he cleared his throat.

Casey reached to put her hand across his. "I don't think so. It's time to move on, son. We have to find a place of our own."

"I really like Matt. I gotta leave Duke too. I promised not to fuss about that, but I wish we could stay."

Had he guessed that she and Matt had become so close? When she looked at him all she saw was an innocent question by a little boy who had found a new friend.

"I know. I like him too. I like Paco and Carmela and wish you could keep your puppy, but that's not real life."

He stood and moved away from her hand, toward the door to the cabin. "Sometimes I hate real life!"

Casey sat for a long time alone, relieved that the snow had finally slacked off and dwindled to a few flakes in the gentle wind. When she went indoors, Jake was lying on his stomach in front of the fireplace, playing with his puppy instead of his computer games. That was an improvement, she decided. Unfortunately, it wouldn't last long. She wanted to talk to him some more, but the expression on his face closed her out. She respected that. He hadn't said more than a few words about his visit to the main house.

It was time to fix lunch anyway. She went into the kitchen and sliced the homemade bread Carmela had sent back with Jake and the puppy. They would have French toast and bacon for lunch, which always cheered him up. The more wholesome, nutritious food could wait a day.

It wouldn't be long at all though, before she had to ask him to return the puppy.

CHAPTER 23

Matt sat on horseback, gazing up at the sky. The first snow was going to stop soon. It never lasted long. He still had many things to do to get ready for winter. He missed his father. They worked well together. Paco was a help, but he wasn't so spry anymore.

Maybe when he turned sixty himself, he would be glad to sit by the fire, dozing. Hell, Paco might have been seventy or eighty for all he knew. No one had ever presumed to ask. Ever since Matt was Jake's age, he had considered Paco older than the hills surrounding the ranch.

He hit his knees gently against the horse's side and reined him toward the arroyo. Better check for strays. It would be easy to track them with the new snow. Once down at the bottom, he checked automatically in the direction of the box canyon where the tumbleweeds piled up. She hadn't written any notes for a long time, why would she now? Did she suspect that he found them?

As if against his will, he urged the horse in that direction and once there, saw the white glare from inside a snow-dusted weed. He leaped from the saddle and with his gloved hand, pushed away the thorny brush to remove the note.

There were two pieces of paper, both dampened by the snow. First, he saw Jake's drawing of the puppy. He wanted Jake to have something of his own, something to love and play with, but he hadn't counted on them leaving. All he did was to make it harder on Jake now that he would have to leave Duke behind. He hadn't thought for one minute that Jake was allergic to animal fur. Hell, the boy rode all that way on horseback without a sign of a problem. It was a wonder Casey hadn't noticed the error of her logic, or didn't she want to?

His throat tightened. He swallowed hard, looking at Jake's picture. Jake had a gift, for sure.

He unfolded the other piece of paper more slowly, treasuring every moment of suspense. When he finished reading Casey's poem, he sat down on a nearby rock and pondered it.

'I thought that love had passed me by, and never would return.
'It came and went so quickly that, I thought I'd never earn...
'a second chance.
'A lifeless, soul-less creature I, had been for many years.
'I'd lost the power to feel, to care...Who was I, with bitter tears,
'to have a second chance?
'But there it is and here am I, just like a fool to let it go.

'Dreaming dreams that can't come true, waiting for my Knight to show.

'Was this my second chance?'

Matt smoothed the note on his thigh and stared at it as if he could wrest the thoughts from the flimsy piece of paper. He put it to his lips, hoping to inhale the faint essence of soap or perfume she wore but smelled only damp dust.

How could he be something he wasn't? He had never done anything romantic in his life. He was pretty sure of that. Adults never acted like teenagers, for any good reason he could think of. Love should fit comfortably, like a familiar pair of boots.

He closed his eyes and felt Casey's softness next to his skin, as if they lay again on the blanket above the mesa, crushing the fragrant grasses underneath their bodies. Unbidden came the remembrance of the sifting gold from between the leaves overhead catching her glorious hair on fire, lighting the length of her body. He almost felt his hand lying on her bare thigh, feeling the pulse and warm moisture of her.

When she surrendered, he guessed it had been the first time she had responded with such passion to anyone. He felt good about that, treasuring the idea she had given a special part of herself to him and him alone.

Adjusting his now too-tight Levis and cramming the papers inside his shirt pocket brought him back to reality. Hellfire, he couldn't go mooning around like a motherless calf. She was set to move away and he knew she wouldn't be back. His life would go on, unchanged.

He rode the horse to the ranch and took out the Jeep. There was only one way to tell.

When he arrived at the cabin, he dashed up the stairs and knocked, impatient to talk to her, now that he had come to a decision.

She came to the door dressed in jeans, a white tee shirt, and big dangling turquoise earrings. He thought he might never find words to speak again.

But he did. "Will you come with me? I've got something to show you."

Casey seemed flustered. The first thing she always did when she was unsettled was to reach her hand up and pat her hair. Odd how that the funny little gesture had grown so dear to him.

"Jake is sleeping. I'm in the middle of—"

Suddenly Jake burst from his room and launched himself at Matt.

"Hey, pard, that's quite a welcome. How did I deserve that?"

Jake pointed toward the packed boxes against the wall. It was then Matt noticed the room had taken on a spare, empty appearance, as if all the light had been removed. Her bright pillows were gone, along with the little touches of silk flowers. The room was flat again, like a bachelor's cabin.

"Come with me. We can leave Jake with Carmela for an hour. I want to show you something."

Jake chattered all the way to the ranch house and they let him fill the void, looking at each other over his head occasionally with indulgent smiles. They watched as Jake and the dog ran toward Carmela. Casey waved and Matt took off down the road. He didn't stop until he parked in front of Dorothy's house.

"Why are we here again?" She remembered the last time he brought her here and the argument that came of it.

"Come inside. One more time." He kept his voice steady, struggling with emotions that he didn't want to get the best of him.

He led the way and she followed him up the steps to wait while he flung the door open.

She stepped inside and gasped.

They watched the sun filter through the open windows, floating on the dust motes disturbed by their entry. He'd emptied the room and removed every stick if furniture, every rug, and left it totally empty

She put her hand on his arm while the silence built around them. The ghosts had gone.

"I—I don't know what to say, Matt. This must have been so hard for you."

"It was—in the beginning. For a time or two I thought I'd better just close the door and forget it. Then..."

She waited, but he felt so uncomfortable, it was hard to finish his words.

"And then?" She prompted.

"This sounds crazy, but it was almost like someone told me it was time to do it. Like someone giving me permission."

"It's not crazy at all. I felt a presence here, too. But I don't now."

He bent his head to look into her eyes. "Does this—does this change anything between us?"

She waited for his words of love, of commitment, of need, but they never came. His look was expectant but carefully devoid of emotion. She shook her head. "It can't. Your feeling for Dorothy was part of the problem, but not all of it."

"I thought that *was* the problem. I don't understand."

"I know you don't and that's the saddest part. You still can't—you can't say things I need to hear."

He didn't know how to answer. Hadn't he shown her what he felt? Wasn't that enough?

"I'm glad you did this, Matthew. It was time. Carmela thought you were holding Dorothy here against her will."

"Carmela told you that?"

Casey nodded. "Carmela loves you very much. You took the place of her son, didn't you know that?"

"No. There's a lot I don't know."

It was difficult for her to look upon this strong, quiet man she loved so much, seeing his soul mirrored in his eyes.

"I didn't suppose Carmela would ever forgive me for her loss, when I never forgave myself." The words were painfully drawn from him. Casey could feel the effort in his voice to keep it steady.

"That's the whole thing. You never forgave yourself. Carmela never blamed you. I know Dorothy wouldn't have either. You know that now, too, don't you?"

The muscles under the skin of his jawline tightened when she touched his arm again. She felt it harden beneath her fingers as he clenched and unclenched his fist.

The healing process had begun. It would continue because Matt was strong and intelligent and he knew she was right.

"Thank you for helping me through this," he finally said, his voice husky.

Still not one word of love. He had apparently decided the issue was closed and he could live without her.

It was then her heart broke exactly in two, sawed neatly in half on dotted lines.

"I'm glad I could help," she said stiffly, trying not to cry. "Now perhaps we'd best get back. I've got more packing to do."

That night, Casey sat on the edge of her bed and let the tears come quietly. She didn't want Jake to hear. Slowly she got up and began putting some things away in a suitcase, things she wouldn't be using in the next week or so. The thought of leaving seemed more substantial that way. Not just some nebulous idea that their leaving might never happen.

She had learned to stand on her own two feet. She learned that the Richards of the world weren't the only choice for a woman. She also knew that no matter how much she loved Matthew Tyree, she could not settle for less than what her heart told her she needed. She wanted to fight for Matt with all her being, but if he didn't love her—if he couldn't love her—there was nothing to fight for.

She brushed the tears from her cheek. It was time she accepted that fact and moved on.

CHAPTER 24

Matt stood at the corral, one booted foot up on the bottom rail. For the first time in a long while he looked at his surroundings and felt a gnawing sense of unrest. His horse, his cattle, the ranch house, all looked the same to him only different. None of this would be worthwhile without Casey. The thought slammed into him with the force of a tornado.

But what could he do? He cleaned out Dorothy's house and exorcised her ghost. He said he would consider the idea of having terminally ill children here to enjoy their last days in sunshine and fresh air. Both Casey and his mom ganged up on him about that.

"Hellfire! I love her and that's the God's honest truth." He spoke out loud to Smokey and the horse ambled closer so he could pet him. The word love stuck on the end of his tongue for a moment and then felt good to say when he said it again. He didn't want her to leave his life. She *was* his life. The realization that he could very well lose her forever weighed heavily.

"Hey, horse. I'm going to ask Carmela. She might know what I'm lacking."

When he went into the house, Carmela wasn't anywhere in sight. He spied a note from her on the kitchen table, saying she and Paco had run into town to pick up a few extra groceries. Damn!

He got in the Jeep and headed down the road to the cabin. He justified the use of his car by thinking that no cowboy would walk when he could ride. Once there at the clearing he sat a while, not knowing how to separate Jake from Casey so he could talk to the boy. Jake had a good head on his shoulders for his age. Maybe he knew what his mother wanted. He slid out from the seat and stood up, leaning against the car.

"Mom! Matt's here!" Jake peeked out the door and then ran down the steps. At the last moment, he skidded to a halt in front of Matt and held out his hand. Like a grown up, Matt was sure the boy told himself. Carefully keeping away the grin that threatened, Matt shook his hand.

By then, Casey had come to the porch and stood watching. Looking up into her eyes, Matt's spirits sank. Her eyes held a cool resolve. She had said what she wanted to say and was ready to leave.

Confused and saddened, he looked up at her. "Morning. I came to see if Jake would like to say good bye to Carmela and Paco and the dogs one more time." Liar, no one was home right now but him. He just didn't know what else to say.

"Fine. I think Jake would like to do that." She looked at Jake. "Okay with you?"

"Yeah, let's go." The boy turned and opened the Jeep door to get in.

"Carmela and Paco aren't here just now, but I wanted to talk to you," Matt said when they were out of earshot.

"Sure. Can we see Smokey? I want to say goodbye to him again, too."

When they pulled up at the driveway, they got out and headed toward the corral. "That's what I wanted to talk to you about, Jake. I don't want a goodbye."

The boy had climbed up on the corral fence and was patting Smokey lightly on his neck. He turned to face Matt. "We don't want a goodbye neither. Why can't we stay here? I told mom I needed a man to man talk with you, but she said not to bother you." His eyes were so like Casey's, Matt wanted to hug him close.

"I'm not sure what to do," Matt confessed. "I don't know what your mom wants from me. I—I love you both very much." There, he'd said the words out loud to another human being.

It promised not to be too difficult once he got the hang of it.

"We love you, too." Jake said, patting Matt's shoulder in a touching gesture of affection.

"It's up to her. Maybe she doesn't want to stay."

"Sure she does. But..." Jake frowned and scratched his head as he had seen Matt do in times of stress.

Matt couldn't help grinning. How great would it be to have a boy like him around all the time.

"You see, you gotta give her stuff. Things."

"Things?"

"Once a friend sent her a card, not for a birthday or anything, just because. And I saw her cry. She said it was a happy cry. Can you write her a poem? She loves poems."

Matt laughed and shook his head. "I don't think so. Anything I did in that sort of thing is bound to make her laugh at me. I don't want that."

"Aw, she wouldn't do that. Anyways, she isn't like us men, 'cause she's a mom. She likes flowers and pretty things. Stuff like that."

Matt took hold of Jake's shoulder, feeling the fragility of his thin frame. The kid needed meat on his bones, sunshine, and lots of outdoors play. Would he get it if they left? "Thanks, pard. I'm going to think on the situation long and hard. But don't give up on me."

After he dropped Jake off at the cabin, Matt decided to drive into Parker. He stopped at the first card shop to ask about a Valentine's card and the clerk told him they were out of season and they didn't have any.

He was not about to give up, even if he had to go to Center City. After the fourth try at card shops and drug stores that lined Parker's main street, the elderly woman behind the counter seemed understanding.

"I know this is crazy, but I have to have a Valentine's card. A big fancy one. Is there any way you can help me?"

The clerk nodded. "I've got a box put away in the storeroom, let me look."

When he selected the perfect card, he made the trip home still pondering. He went inside and sat at his desk. Playing with a pen, he pulled out a pad of paper from a drawer.

Casey had to have something special to change her mind about leaving.

CHAPTER 25

"Mom! Come quick!"

Casey stood on the back porch, shaking out a rug when she heard Jake's shriek. She could tell from the sound she didn't need to be alarmed. This was his excited voice.

She brought the rug inside and laid it down in front of the fireplace. Their bags were packed and leaning against the wall. The day had turned dark and foreboding, as bleak as her thoughts. According to the radio, a winter storm was heading in their direction. They should have gone before now, but inertia had claimed her. She couldn't make decisions or move fast. It was as if her feet were stuck in syrup and her brain along with them.

One thing holding her back was her indecision about telling Matt goodbye. She didn't want to face him, or say the words, and see the shards of her dreams in the expression on his face. Hadn't they in essence already said their goodbyes? What more was there to say? But it wasn't fair just to run off without letting Jake see everyone one last time.

Maybe she should put the goodbye message in a tumbleweed. The thought turned her mouth down in a wry grimace. Forget the tumbleweeds, she was through with that nonsense and wished she never read the book that mentioned doing such a silly thing. She was through writing poetry, too, like some romantic idiot. Grow up, Casey, she admonished herself.

"Hurry, Mom! Hurry!" Jake sounded as if he was jumping up and down on the porch.

Casey opened the screen door, saw both ends, and around the corner of the porch taken up with what appeared to be hundreds of tumbleweeds, many with pieces of paper sticking out of them. "What in the world?"

"It's a humungous bunch of tumblewords. For us. I know it is. See there?" He was nearly hysterical with excitement, dancing up and down, and pointing to a large white square envelope nestled in the middle of a tumbleweed that sat on top of the others on the porch.

She laughed at Jake's delight. What had happened? Did it rain tumbleweeds in Colorado?

The first envelope Jake handed her was covered with big red hand-drawn hearts. In the middle, it said, "I Love You Casey."

All the rest contained little notes saying how he admired her eyes, her hair, and her body. Casey found herself reading carefully now, editing as she went. He was really getting into things and Jake was all ears. Finally, exhausted, she stopped him. "Whoa. Time out. Don't you want to know what's in the biggest envelope?" She pointed at the one resting on top of all the others. "Can you get it out?" she asked.

"You do it. I know it's for you."

Sighing, she reached forward and retrieved the envelope. Jake took her hand and they went to the porch swing to sit. "Read it, Mom. Out loud. I wanna hear."

Casey opened her mouth to read her name on the front of the envelope, but the words blurred in front of her eyes. "Excuse me a minute. I'll read it, just hang in there," she managed, her voice choking up.

Jake leaned back against the porch rail, his arms stretched out behind his head like he'd seen Matt do, waiting.

She opened the envelope and pulled out a huge Valentine card, replete with old-fashioned lacy hearts and flowers and gaudy foldouts. Matt must have gone to Parker and beyond just for this one. He had to have made an extreme effort to get someone to come up with such an out-of-season Valentine card of this style. The words at the bottom of the card brought hot tears to Casey's eyes and for a moment she couldn't swallow, let alone read aloud.

"Grow old along with me, the best is yet to be.
The last of life for which the first was made."

Browning said it much better than I ever could.
I love you, Casey, with all my heart and soul.

I want and need you in my life forever.

Matt

The most beautiful love words ever written along with his own words, the words she thought never to hear from him. Casey bent her head over her lap and began to sob. All the frustrations of the past months, all the loneliness of the past years, all gathered inside her and poured out. She cried until at last she felt empty enough to be able to stop.

When she finished crying, she felt the light touch of Jake's hand on her back, gently patting her. Had she frightened him? She raised her head. Her tears blurred his face, but he grinned, his eyes lit in that magical way she loved.

"It's okay, Mom. He said you'd probably cry and that I shouldn't worry."

"*He* said?"

Jake grinned. "He couldn't say the words he wrote. I don't know why. I told him to write you a poem. I said you might need a poem. That was his idea to put it in the tumblewords." Jake sounded smugly pleased with himself.

"You talked about this and knew he was going to do something but kept it a secret? When?"

Jake laughed. "When I went to tell them goodbye again, me and Matt had a man to man talk."

Casey felt such a surge of love for her son and for Matt that she didn't know if she could hold it all inside. Jake began to giggle and Casey, tears dried, laughed with him.

"Look!" Jake pointed toward the yard and she watched Matt ride up on his horse.

Suddenly the day was so blindingly bright as if the lowering snow clouds had disappeared. Her problems were still with her. But she and Matt would have each other to share both the good times and the bad. Someone to ride the river with.

His bold silhouette, the set to his wide shoulders, and the strong, brown hands holding the reins made her heart sing. She knew now that chiseled-in-granite profile hid a romantic soul.

Casey hugged Jake to her and kissed the top of his head. "Come on, kiddo. What are we waiting for?

They ran down the steps to welcome the man they both loved.

THE END

About The Author

Born in Phoenix, Arizona, Pinkie Paranya traveled all over the U.S., Alaska, and most of Mexico with her late husband. Ever since she can remember, writing has been her passion. After completing her fifteenth novel, trying to discover the genre she loved most, she still hasn't decided.

Paranya enjoys romances with their intrigue and uplifting happy endings, but she has also published two paranormal psychological suspenses, a cozy mystery, and an Early American Alaskan trilogy. To date, she has thirteen published novels.

Visit her website, www.pinkieparanya.com.

CPSIA information can be obtained at www.ICGtesting.com
Printed in the USA
LVOW110859190312

273731LV00001B/48/P